catch us
if you can

by Hope McLean

Scholastic Inc.

For Holly O'Connor, who loves shiny, sparkly gems as much as she loves history. — H.M.

ISBN 978-0-545-60762-9

12 11 10 9 8 7 6 5 4 3 2   14 15 16 17/0

Printed in the U.S.A.   40
This edition first printing, June 2013
Previously published as *Jewel Thieves: Catch Us if You Can*
Book design by Natalie C. Sousa

Chapter One

Willow Albern gripped the buzzer in her hand, anxious to hear the next question. Across the room, the four members of the Franklin Middle School Owls looked like lions ready to pounce. She could feel her heart beating in her chest; her team had to get the next question right — or lose the match.

The Martha Washington Jewels were thirty points behind the Owls, and Willow knew that this was the last ten-point toss-up question. To win, the Jewels would have to get it right, plus the thirty-point bonus question that followed.

The quiz bowl moderator, a tall, thin man in a gray suit, adjusted his eyeglasses and read the card in his hand.

"This next question is a Math question," he announced. "Find the value of eight cubed, or eight to the third power."

Willow quickly did the calculations in her head and pressed the buzzer. The moderator nodded at her, acknowledging that she had buzzed in first.

"Five hundred and twelve," Willow answered confidently.

"That is correct," the moderator replied, and a small wave of applause swept through the crowd of friends, family members, and fellow quiz bowl contestants who filled the Franklin Middle School auditorium.

"Nice one," whispered her teammate Jasmine Johnson, and Willow flashed her a smile.

"Your bonus question is three parts worth ten points each," the moderator announced. "The Jewels must answer all three questions correctly to win the match."

Willow's palms started to sweat. This was it. Gazing out into the audience, she saw her mom sitting next to Jasmine's parents. Mrs. Albern gave her daughter a thumbs-up, and Willow felt a wave of confidence flow through her. They could do this.

Across the stage, the Franklin Owls were finally starting to get nervous. They had walked into the competition expecting to beat the Jewels, who were new to the Washington, DC–area quiz bowl circuit. But the sixth-grade girls were tougher than they looked.

Many of the teams competing in the tournament that day were from other prep schools or private schools, so they wore their school uniforms. Other squads wore matching T-shirts. But since Martha Washington hadn't had a quiz bowl team in years, the Jewels didn't have cool uniforms or intimidating outfits. They hadn't even had a chance to coordinate their look yet.

Willow was the team captain, and she liked to be comfortable when competing — both on and off the field. Today, she wore a sporty T-shirt, a short denim skirt, and sneakers. Willow was tall and thin, with dark hazel eyes and brown skin. She wore her long hair in neat braids that she tied into a ponytail, so she wouldn't be distracted. Willow looked over at her teammates.

Jasmine stood next to her. She was an inch shorter than Willow, but her wild curly hair made her look a little bit taller. A purple headband tried to tame her light brown curls, and she was dressed like a dancer in her favorite black leggings and a long, purple knit top. The two girls looked like complete opposites, but Jasmine and Willow had one thing in common: They both wanted to be the top scorer on the Jewels team.

Beside Jasmine, Lili Higashida had woven strands of fake pink hair into her glossy black bob. "For luck!" she had explained, peppily. Her polka-dotted top should have clashed with her skirt and striped tights, but somehow the outfit worked, like Lili's styles always did.

The last team member, Erin Fischer, had woken up late. Having thrown on a "Save the Earth" T-shirt and jeans, then briefly run a comb through her frizzy strawberry blond hair, she managed to make it out to her driveway about two minutes before Willow's mom had picked them all up that morning.

No, they definitely did *not* have a team look going on.

"The theme of this bonus question is China, the country," the moderator said. "You will have five seconds to answer each part. Part one: What green gem has been prized by the Chinese for centuries?"

The Jewels quickly huddled together to discuss their response, but Jasmine had the answer ready. Nobody on the team knew gems and minerals the way she did.

"Jade!" Jasmine whispered. Willow, as the team captain, swiftly repeated the answer into the microphone.

"Correct!" the moderator announced. "And now for part two. Invented in China, this fabric is made from the cocoon woven by the larva of a moth."

Willow panicked for a second. Lili was supposed to be their expert on the arts, music, and literature, but Willow still wasn't sure how much she knew. This was Lili's first year at Martha Washington School, and the rest of the Jewels were just getting to know her. Then Willow saw Lili smile.

"That's easy. It's silk," Lili said.

"Silk," Willow repeated, after rushing back to the microphone.

"Correct," said the moderator. "The score is now tied. Jewels, here is your third part, for the win. What mountain range can be found on the southwest border of China?"

Willow turned to Erin, the team's history and geography expert. Her pale cheeks were flushed bright red, like they always were when she answered a question. But her voice was confident when she replied.

"It's the Himalayas."

Willow glanced at the other girls, who all nodded. They trusted Erin.

"The Himalayas!" Willow answered.

The moderator smiled. "Correct! This match goes to the Jewels of Martha Washington School."

Erin and Lili started screaming and jumping up and down. Jasmine hugged Willow.

"Um, guys?" Willow interrupted the team's celebrations. "I think we're supposed to shake hands with the other team." She nodded in the direction of the Franklin Owls.

The girls quickly calmed down and followed Willow across the stage, where they shook hands with each of the crestfallen Owls.

"There will be a ten-minute break until the next round," the moderator announced.

The Jewels climbed down from the stage and were greeted by their parents, who gave them all big hugs. Then they headed outside to take a break. They were done for the day, but they planned on sticking around to watch the other teams compete.

They found a row of vending machines near the main entrance to the school, and each girl got a bottle of water. Erin bought a giant Choco-Blast bar, too. Willow looked at her with a raised eyebrow.

"You know, I have an extra granola bar in my backpack," she told Erin, who was already tearing through the wrapper.

"Thanks, but chocolate is the best way to celebrate," Erin replied with a grin. "Besides, I need an energy boost. That was pretty intense!"

The girls nodded in agreement as they sat down on the school steps. It was a Saturday afternoon, and even though Franklin's regular students weren't on campus, the steps were still crowded with other teams enjoying the break. It was a crisp fall day, and the air was just chilly enough to feel welcome after the girls had been cooped up in the stuffy auditorium. It was getting cooler, though, and the first orange rays of the late afternoon were beginning to stream through the branches of the surrounding trees, setting the leaves aglow.

"I actually think it was fun," said Lili. "I'm glad you convinced me to join the team, Willow."

"And I'm glad you joined," Willow said. "None of us can handle those art history questions. Plus you've got all the literature and music stuff down, too."

"And you're generally awesome," Erin added. The girls giggled.

"And anyway, Principal Frederickson is the one who told me to ask you," Willow said. "I think she handpicked all of us. She said that Martha Washington hasn't had an academic team in years, and she wanted the best of the best."

"So why did she pick *us*?" Erin joked, and Lili nudged her in the ribs.

Lili took a phone from the pink velvet pouch she had tied around her waist.

"I've got to text Mom. She's not going to believe this!"

The rest of the girls took out their phones and started spreading the good news. A moment later, a boy's voice sounded from behind them.

"Not bad — for a first try."

The Jewels turned to see a boy wearing a black prep-school uniform and a blue tie standing on the step above them. He was tall for his age, with wavy blond hair.

"Um, thanks!" Willow replied nervously.

The boy grinned and walked to the auditorium entrance, where his three teammates waited for him. Between their matching uniforms and haughty smirks, Willow couldn't help feeling intimidated.

She turned back to her friends. "Oh my gosh, I can't believe it!"

"Is that who I think it was?" Jasmine asked.

"Yep. Ryan Atkinson, the captain of the Atkinson Prep Rivals. And he just gave us a compliment!" Willow said, a little starstruck. "*Sort of* a compliment, anyway. Those guys are, like, legendary. An Atkinson team has won the national championships for the last five years in a row. I just can't believe they noticed us!"

"Wait a second," Erin said. "Why is his name the same as the school?"

"His family founded the school, like, hundreds of years ago," Lili explained. "His uncle is the principal. I know 'cause my brother, Eli, goes to Atkinson."

"They're all super snooty, if you ask me," Erin remarked. "You know, I wonder why we didn't see them at sign-in this morning."

Willow shrugged. "I guess they showed up just in time for their match. They probably don't need to scope out the other teams like most of us do. Everyone says they can't be beat."

Jasmine's eyes narrowed. "We'll see about that. We're off to a pretty good start."

"Yeah," Lili agreed. "Besides, their uniforms are boring."

"I kind of like them," Willow admitted. "It makes them look . . . serious. I was thinking maybe we should get some uniforms."

Lili got a gleam in her eyes. "Ooh, I could design them! I'm thinking . . . matching tutus, maybe?"

Jasmine laughed and shook her head. "Willow wants us to look serious, not *fabulous*, Lili!"

"Well, maybe the tutus could be plaid," Lili suggested. "Plaid is very school-like. Very serious."

"Oh, I know," Erin said. "How about T-shirts that say 'Jewels Rule!' "

"Nice, but not exactly what I was thinking," Willow replied.

"But that would be serious," Erin argued. "Seriously *awesome*."

"Well, maybe we should just wear our regular clothes for now," Willow suggested.

"It doesn't matter what we wear, as long as we're good," Jasmine agreed. "Anyway, we've got to keep winning. We've got to show the other schools that the Martha Washington Jewels are here to stay."

"Yeah, we were awesome today," Erin said. "That question about the Himalayas was a no-brainer. It's only, like, the highest mountain range in the whole world. And nice job with the silk, Lili."

"I love silk," Lili said. "It's so soft and beautiful — even if it *is* made by worms."

"Larvae, technically," Jasmine corrected her.

"Oh, right," Lili said. "See? I'm not so good at the science stuff."

"That's why we're the perfect team," Willow remarked. "We're each good at something different."

She jumped to her feet.

"Team cheer!" she commanded, and the girls formed a circle.

"Math!" Willow cried, placing her hand in the center.

Laying her hand on top of Willow's, Jasmine yelled, "Science!"

"History!" Erin added next.

Lili slapped her hand on top of Erin's. "Um . . . art, literature, and stuff!" The girls laughed, and Lili shrugged. "I'm working on it."

Then they all cheered together.

"Goooooo Jewels!"

As they raised their hands in the air to end the cheer, a woman with blond hair ran up to them. It was Ms. Keatley, their team advisor.

"She must be coming to congratulate us," Erin guessed.

But as their advisor got closer, the girls noticed the worried look on her face.

"Ms. Keatley, what's wrong?" Erin asked. The Jewels gathered around.

"Oh, girls, it's just terrible!" the teacher said. "The Martha Washington ruby has been stolen!"

Chapter Two

"Oh my gosh!" Jasmine cried. "Not the ruby!"

"When? How? Who?" Erin asked.

"Honestly, I'm not sure," Ms. Keatley replied. "Principal Frederickson just noticed it was missing from the library. And I'm friends with Mrs. Potter, the librarian, and she just texted me. So I guess it happened between when school closed last night and this afternoon."

The teacher's cell phone rang, and she looked at the screen. "It's Mrs. Potter again. I'd better get this."

The girls looked at one another, stunned, as Ms. Keatley walked away.

"It doesn't seem real," Lili said. "Weird, right?"

The girls were speechless. The ruby, which had once belonged to Martha Washington herself, was set in a beautiful gold necklace. It was always kept in a locked glass case inside the library reading room, where every student could enjoy it. It was the unofficial heart of the school — and inspired its official mascot, the ruby-throated hummingbird. The Fighting Rubies had represented Martha Washington School's sports teams for generations. And the Jewels had used the first letter of each of their own names to make up their quiz bowl team, in honor of the ruby: Jasmine, Erin, Willow, Lili. Every girl on campus was proud to have the gem in their school.

"Well, it was a valuable piece," Willow reasoned. "Maybe a jewel thief stole it so they could sell it?"

"It was a valuable piece of *history*, too," Erin pointed out. "Maybe some Martha Washington fanatic took it."

Willow looked skeptical. "George Washington, maybe, but are people really fanatical about Martha?"

"Hey, people always overlook women in history," Erin said. "I'm just saying. There could be some Martha-obsessed people out there."

Lili gave a little shudder. "I don't know. It feels kind of personal, you know? Like somebody's out to get our school."

Jasmine was pale. "This is just awful!" she said, tearing up.

"Well, yeah, but it's just a ruby, right?" Erin said.

"Well, yes, but . . ." Jasmine stopped with a sigh. Erin gave her a quick hug, sensing her friend was taking the theft a little harder than the rest of them.

Jasmine knew it was just a pretty rock, but she had always thought it was special. She imagined going to the library on Monday and seeing the empty case. In a weird way, it felt like losing a friend.

Maybe it was because she had gone to Martha Washington since kindergarten, but the ruby was Jasmine's favorite gem. And for a "geology nut" (as Willow called her), that was saying a lot. On her twelfth birthday her parents had given her a pair of ruby earrings, two tiny red stones on silver posts. They were the prize of her collection, which Jasmine had started as soon as she was old enough to hold a rock in her hand. Her samples were neatly organized in boxes and bins in her room and included everything from polished brown pieces of agate to silvery gray chunks of zinc.

But nothing in her collection compared to the Martha Washington ruby necklace, which was made up of thirteen rubies set in burnished gold. The necklace would have been special just because it belonged to Martha Washington, but the center ruby was truly stunning — as large as a penny and the deep color of a rose.

"I'm sure the police will find who did it," Willow said, comfortingly.

"And if they don't, Principal Frederickson will," Erin said. Then she gave a mock shudder. "I'd hate to be the criminal when Principal Frederickson finds him. She's scarier than the Terminator."

"She sure is," Jasmine said, forcing a smile for her friends.

"Goooooo Willow!" Erin yelled the next day as she stamped her feet on the bleachers.

Lili grinned. "*This* is how you do it," she said as she held her thumb and index finger together, then placed them in her mouth. She inhaled deeply before letting out a piercing whistle.

The other people sitting in the bleachers turned to look at them.

Jasmine wiggled uncomfortably on the bench. "Would you guys knock it off?" she said. "Everyone is staring at us!"

"Relax, Jasmine," Lili giggled. "We're just showing our support for Willow and the Martha Washington Rubies."

"We're *loudly* showing our support," Erin said before she yelled, "Goooooo Rubies!"

Jasmine sighed and leaned forward, putting her chin in her hands. Erin looked over her friend's all-black outfit.

"What's up, Jazz? No Ruby red today?" Erin pointed to her own red Martha Washington sweatshirt.

"I'm in mourning," Jasmine said. "For the ruby."

"Ooh, I could make you a hat with a black veil," Lili said. "Totally goth." Erin stifled a laugh.

"I am not goth," Jasmine protested. "Just sad."

"Well, cheer up, because we *goth* to cheer for Willow now," Erin joked. "Go team!"

The bleachers overlooked a soccer field. The Fighting Rubies were playing the Blue Knights, the Atkinson Prep girls' soccer team. Willow, wearing the team's ruby-red-and-white uniform, was easy to spot. She stood a few inches taller than most of her teammates.

The Rubies controlled the ball, and the Knights chased after the Martha Washington midfielders as they quickly passed the ball along toward Atkinson territory. With a swift kick, Willow launched the ball right to the Rubies' forward, who charged toward the goal.

"Way to go, Willow!" Erin yelled, and Willow looked up into the stands and waved. As she did, an Atkinson player with short blond hair ran down the field and shoved right into her! Willow lost her balance and tumbled onto the green turf. With a mocking smile, the blonde looked up into the bleachers and waved to the Jewels before sauntering away.

Erin's face grew bright red. "Did you see that?" she asked Jasmine and Lili. "She did that on purpose! Willow didn't even have the ball."

Jasmine frowned. "She made sure the ref's back was turned. I know her. That's Isabel Baudin. She's one of the Atkinson Prep Rivals — the French girl."

"You're right. I recognize her from yesterday's meet," Erin said. "She was waiting for Ryan Atkinson on the steps."

"I've heard she's one of the main reasons why the other quiz bowl teams can't stand the Rivals," Jasmine said.

"Why is that?" Lili asked.

"The Rivals are really smart, obviously. But I've gotten the impression that they're not very nice — especially Isabel," Jasmine confided. "I was talking to Maddie, one of the Owls, at yesterday's quiz bowl. After the Rivals beat them at a match a couple of weeks ago, and it was time to shake hands, Isabel made fun of Maddie for not knowing the answer to one of the questions. It was totally uncalled for. And Maddie said Isabel's done it to other competitors, too."

"Mean people stink." Lili sighed. "What's the point of acting that way?"

Jasmine shrugged. "It could be an intimidation thing. The next time the Owls face the Rivals, they'll remember not only getting beat, but getting teased, too. For some reason, I think insults sound worse in a French accent."

Erin shook her head vigorously. "That wouldn't work with me," she said. "No way. It would make me want to beat them even more the next time we squared off."

"Everyone is different," Jasmine replied. "And Lili is proof of that!" Jasmine pointed at her friend, who was wearing a "Fighting Rubies" T-shirt with black tights and a red, black, and white plaid tutu that she had created from strips of tulle.

Lili laughed. "Come on. Wouldn't this make an amazing uniform for quiz bowl?"

"That reminds me, Mom is going to kill you when you get home," a voice said. A high-school-age boy in the blue-and-black Atkinson soccer uniform had climbed up the bleachers. His jet-black hair was layered and styled in short spikes on top of his head.

"Eli! What are you doing here?" Lili asked.

"I must have told you twenty times that my freshman match was being held here this afternoon," Eli explained. "Anyway, Mom was going to use that tulle for the floral arrangements at Aunt Kei's party tonight. She had to go out and get some more."

"How did she know that I took it?" Lili said.

"Oh, I don't know. Maybe the trail of red, black, and white tulle that led from her workroom to your closet?" Eli suggested with a smile.

Lili dramatically put her hand on her forehead. "When artistic inspiration strikes, I must create!"

Eli rolled his eyes before grinning at Jasmine and Erin. "Hi, girls. So, I heard about that stolen ruby. That's too bad."

Jasmine moaned, burying her head in her hands. Eli looked confused.

"Jasmine had a psychic connection to the ruby or something," Erin informed him. "Don't ask."

Eli shrugged. "Okay. How's the game going?"

"They're tied, but I'm not feeling too friendly toward anyone in an Atkinson uniform right now," Erin admitted, nodding at his jersey. "It's too bad you can't be a Fighting Ruby!"

"Since Martha Washington is an all-girls school, that would be kinda difficult," Eli said. "But what's with all the Atkinson anger, guys?"

Jasmine told Eli how Isabel had shoved Willow on the field. Eli looked thoughtful. Just then, the crowd let out a groan. "Hey, ref, are you blind?" a man yelled out.

"It was that Isabel again!" Erin was indignant. "She elbowed Willow. And she keeps making sure to do it *only* when the referee isn't looking."

"My throat is dry from all that whistling. I need some water," Lili said. "Eli, I don't have any money with me. Can you lend me some?"

Eli reached into the pocket of his shorts. "Luckily I'm always looking out for my little sister. I guess plaid tutus don't have pockets, huh?"

"Eli, you're the best!" Lili beamed at her brother. "And don't worry, I'll patch things up with Mom when I get home. I promise."

"You better! Otherwise she'll be in a bad mood all week," Eli said.

Lili turned to Erin and Jasmine. "Be right back," she said.

"Wait for me!" Erin called out, following Lili down the stairs. "I need a bag of Cheezy Bites to calm me down."

The two girls walked down the bleachers and along the field, toward the Snack Shack. The small building was a favorite hangout for students during games.

"Do you think Willow's mom is working at the Shack today?" Erin asked.

With that, they heard Mrs. Albern's loud, distinctive laugh. Willow's mom was well known to everyone in the Hallytown area. She ran the local community center, and anyone who took a class there knew her.

"Girls! Come on over, let me get you something to eat. I heard it's been a pretty rough game today for Willow," Mrs. Albern said.

"It has been! That girl Isabel is deliberately going after her," Erin complained.

"I may be her mom, but I'm not biased when I say Willow's one of the best players on the team. That makes her a target," she sighed, brushing a stray braid out of her face. Her dark hair was braided like Willow's, but she wore hers coiled into an elegant bun. "Willow was pretty upset about that stolen ruby, too. I'm sure all you girls are."

"Jasmine's the most upset," Erin told her. "I don't know. I guess it feels weird that somebody actually broke into the school and stole something."

"Yeah," Lili agreed. "It's like the trust is gone. Who knows what someone will take next?" She gasped. "I can't remember if I locked up my locker over the weekend. Oh no!"

Mrs. Albern nodded sympathetically. "I'm sure your locker is fine, Lili, but I understand how you feel," she said. "It can be very unnerving to be robbed. Anyway, can you please give these to Willow when you see her?" Mrs. Albern slipped a box of red licorice into Erin's hand. "She likes to act tough, but she's going to need these after the game to cheer her up."

"Sure thing, Mrs. Albern," Erin replied.

Lili looked puzzled. "Hey, I thought Willow was all healthy and stuff."

"She is, but this is the only candy she can't resist," Erin explained.

"It's like her kryptonite." Mrs. Albern smiled.

Lili got a bottle of water, and instead of the Cheezy Bites, Erin bought some nachos to share. As the girls headed back to the bleachers they passed by the Fighting Rubies, who were in a huddle on the sidelines.

"Stay strong, Willow!" Erin called as she and Lili climbed back up the bleachers to sit with Jasmine and Eli. She waved the licorice in the air.

Willow lifted her head and smiled at the sight of her friends. She was pretty frustrated; Isabel had been elbowing and pushing her every chance she got.

"You've got to take that girl out," a teammate said to Willow. "You're the only one of us who can pull off a slide tackle."

"A slide tackle? That's a little underhanded," she replied, confused.

"That girl has it coming. She's been clocking you all game," another teammate commented. "We'll lose if she keeps cheating."

Willow thought carefully about it. To perform a slide tackle, she would have to slide into the ball, *then* into the person in possession of the ball. If Willow hit the ball first and Isabel second, it was a legal move. But if she slid into Isabel first, she could get called for a penalty. The score was still tied.

"If I get a chance, I will," she told her teammates. "Sometimes you have to fight fire with fire."

The Rubies ran onto the field. The Atkinson team quickly took possession of the ball. Someone passed it to Isabel. Willow stayed right with her until they were just outside the goal area. Willow went in for the slide tackle, aiming carefully for the ball. Isabel caught on to what she was doing and jumped over the ball, blocking it with her body. Already in motion, it was too late for Willow to stop. She crashed into Isabel. The referee blew his whistle and called a penalty on Willow.

"Nice try," Isabel said in her lilting French accent as she grabbed the ball. The penalty allowed her to place the ball anywhere she wanted before taking the shot.

As Isabel set the ball down in front of the net, Willow could hear jeers streaming out over the field from the Martha Washington bleachers. Isabel lined up her shot, and a swift, determined kick sent the ball sailing toward the net.

Goal! The game was over. Atkinson had beaten Martha Washington by one point.

Willow lined up with her team to shake hands with the Atkinson players. "Good game, good game," everyone repeated to one another. Willow had to take a deep breath when it was her turn to shake Isabel's hand.

Isabel smiled at Willow, her green eyes gleaming. "You almost had me," she said. "But I am too quick for you!"

"You're too much of a cheater for me," Willow said calmly, looking her square in the eyes.

"But I'm the winner, no?" Isabel asked with a smile before letting go of Willow's hand and moving down the line. Willow shook her head as she left the field.

"That was so unfair!" Erin cried as the Jewels rushed up to Willow on the sidelines.

"You played a great game," Lili said. "I'm proud of you."

Erin handed her the box of red licorice, and Willow took out a strand. She munched on the candy as she thought things over.

"It's not losing that bothers me; it's losing to *her*." Willow looked over at Isabel, who was the center of a giant team hug on the Blue Knights' sidelines. "How are we supposed to win anything when we're up against cheaters?"

Jasmine met her eyes. "I know I've been upset about the ruby — we all are — but we've got to keep it together," she said, looking like her normal self for the first time in twenty-four hours. "It's a long quiz bowl season, and we're off to a good start. We've just got to keep winning, that's all." She gave Willow a friendly nudge. "And we've got to beat those Rivals!"

Chapter Three

The next morning, Lili's mom dropped her off in front of the school, as always. Even though it had been two months since she'd started, Lili still couldn't get over how pretty her new school was. Each of the three buildings was made of stone, and green ivy climbed up the walls. Bright orange and purple mums lined the walkways, and the maple trees on the lawn were just beginning to turn a warm shade of red.

When she got out of the car she saw Willow, Jasmine, and Erin on the front steps. Willow was angrily shaking her phone.

"Did you see Isabel's Chatter post?" she asked her friends. "It says, 'So happy! The Knights destroyed the Rubies on the field!' Can you believe that?"

"That stinks!" Erin agreed. "If I had a Chatter page, I'd post something about how she cheated."

"You should do it, Willow," Jasmine urged. "You have a Chatter account, right?"

Willow shook her head. "I do, but the refs didn't see what she did. If I post that, it'll sound like I'm a sore loser. The best thing is to ignore it."

"I don't know how you do it, Willow," Jasmine remarked. "I'd be so angry I couldn't stop myself."

"Yoga," Willow replied. She raised her arms over her head, pressed her palms together, and then brought her hands down in front of her chest. "It's totally relaxing. You guys really need to come to class with me sometime."

Erin shook her head. "I don't know. Is it really relaxing to be . . ."

She was interrupted by two police cars pulling into the parking lot. Their sirens were off, but they still looked ominous.

"Do you think they're here about the ruby?" Lili asked.

"They must be investigating the theft," Willow said.

"Great! I'm glad someone is looking for it. With the police involved, maybe they'll find it."

"I hope so," Jasmine said.

As much as she tried, Jasmine just couldn't stop thinking about the ruby. When her last class ended that day she went to the library to do homework, but the police tape across the door to the reading room just made her sad all over again. She took out her math notebook, and instead of doing her work, she took some colored pencils out of her bag and began to sketch the necklace from memory.

"Hey, that's pretty good!" a voice said. Jasmine jumped. It was Willow, looking at the sketch over her shoulder.

"You scared me!" Jasmine said. "But anyway, thanks. I don't think I can get the color right, though. It's hard to recreate that deep red."

"It was really beautiful," Willow agreed.

"Did you know that the red color in a ruby comes from chromium?" Jasmine asked. "That's the same stuff they add to iron to make stainless steel."

"Wow," Willow said. "That's pretty cool."

"The deeper red the ruby is, the more valuable it is," Jasmine added. "So I bet Martha's was worth a fortune."

"That's probably why it got stolen," Willow reasoned. "Anyway, I came to talk to you about something. I had Ms. Keatley email me the video of our matches this weekend, and I kept track of the answers we got wrong and then charted them."

"For fun?" Jasmine asked. "Wow, you are, like, quiz bowl–crazy these days."

Willow shrugged. "I just want us to win, okay? Sports teams review their tapes, so I figured we should, too." She hesitated, like she wasn't sure if she should say what was coming next. "Anyway, I figured out that our weakest areas are technology and astronomy."

The words hit Jasmine like a bee sting. She was supposed to be the Jewels' science expert.

"So what are you saying? That I'm the weakest teammate?" she asked defensively.

"No way!" Willow protested. "Science has so many branches, and you can't expect to be an expert in all of them by yourself. You're already amazing at chemistry, biology, and geology."

"Yes, I am," Jasmine agreed. The girls had known each other since kindergarten, and Willow knew just what to say to make her friend feel better.

"So I'm thinking that we *all* need to brush up on our technology as a team," Willow continued. "We could take a field trip to the National Air and Space Museum."

"That could be fun," Jasmine admitted.

Erin and Lili came into the library and walked over.

"Did you tell her?" Erin asked.

Willow rolled her eyes. "Nice. Way to be subtle. But yes, I told her, and she's cool."

"Of *course* I'm cool," Jasmine insisted.

Then Erin noticed the sketch in her notebook. "Nice work, Jasmine! You know, since the ruby got taken I've been trying to find out more about it. Mostly I'm just learning about Martha Washington. I've borrowed a ton of old books about her from the library. Did you know that she was the oldest of eight brothers and sisters?"

"No," Jasmine said. "I don't actually know much about her. Except that she had good taste in jewelry."

"I don't think we'll be getting a lot of Martha Washington questions at quiz bowl," Willow pointed out.

"Well, you never know," Erin told her. "Besides, not everything we do has to be about quiz bowl, does it?"

Willow didn't answer. Ever since they had created the team, quiz bowl had been the only thing on her mind, but she didn't want her friends to think she was weird or anything.

"Hey, we should talk to Ms. Keatley and set up that trip," she suggested.

"And then can we ask her about that fashion makeover I want to do on her?" Lili asked.

"We'll hurt her feelings, Lili," Willow protested.

Lili sighed. "We'd be doing her a favor. She's so pretty she could be on TV if she wanted to. But it's like she puts on a blindfold in the morning and just randomly picks stuff out of her closet."

"She's an *intellectual*," Erin said, popping a loud bubble with her gum. "They're too busy thinking to care about what they're wearing."

"Fine," Lili said. "I'll just wait till the right moment, that's all."

The girls found Ms. Keatley grading papers in her history classroom. She looked up, startled, and brushed a strand of hair away from her face.

"Is today a practice day?" she asked. "I thought it was Monday."

"It is Monday," Willow assured her. "We just wanted to ask you if we could go on a field trip to the National Air and Space Museum this weekend. To brush up on our technology."

"That's a great idea!" Ms. Keatley started sorting through the papers on her desk. "Yes, here are those statistics you worked up. Nicely done, Willow. You girls certainly have a lot of initiative."

"Can we go on Saturday?" Willow asked. "We don't have a quiz bowl match this weekend."

"Well, I was planning to watch the all-day marathon of the John Adams miniseries, but I do have it on DVD. . . ." she said thoughtfully. "And it's wonderful that you girls want to broaden your horizons. You know, if you make it to nationals, living in the DC area will be a terrific advantage. There are so many great museums and resources here."

"You mean, *when* we make it to nationals," Willow corrected her.

Ms. Keatley smiled and shook her head. "I'll email your parents and arrange the trip for Saturday."

Willow pumped her fist in the air. "Yes! Those Rivals won't stand a chance."

Erin laughed. "Admit it, Willow. You're obsessed!"

Chapter Four

The next morning, Jasmine and Lili were in Biology class together, watching a film about cell division. The room was dark, and the film flickered on a screen in the front of the room. Normally Jasmine would have taken detailed notes, but today she just felt like drawing another picture of the necklace in her notebook.

She was shading the large ruby when she felt a tap on her shoulder. Startled, she looked up to see her Biology teacher, Ms. Virani, standing next to her.

"Principal Frederickson would like to see you in her office," she whispered.

Jasmine quickly gathered her books and made her way out of the classroom. Lili looked at her with raised eyebrows, but Jasmine just shrugged. She honestly didn't know what was going on. Why would the principal want to see her? She had never gotten detention once in her whole school career; she'd never even been late.

She walked through the school's spotless hallways to the main office, where the school secretary greeted her.

"You can go right in," Ms. Ortiz said, nodding toward the principal's door.

When she stepped inside, Jasmine was surprised to see her mom sitting in one of the red leather chairs in front of the principal's desk.

"Is everything okay?" she asked, running to her mom. For a split second, she thought maybe something horrible had happened at home.

"Principal Frederickson called this morning and asked if your father or I could come down. Your dad's working, so here I am." Mrs. Johnson was a private music teacher, and her workday didn't begin until three o'clock, when kids got out of school. She turned to Principal Frederickson with a quizzical look. "But I'm not sure what this is all about."

Relieved, Jasmine took the seat next to her mother. Principal Frederickson still hadn't said anything. She looked as stern as ever, with her perfectly curled dark hair, crisp white blouse, and black blazer. Jasmine couldn't help noticing the shiny brooch she wore on her lapel. Were those emeralds?

Jasmine wanted to like Principal Frederickson, since she had brought the Jewels together, but she actually found her kind of scary.

She was the whole reason Jasmine's family had sent her to Martha Washington in the first place. She was a graduate of the school, too.

"I want you to have the influence of a strong woman in your life as you're growing up," her grandmother always said.

"But I have you and Mom," Jasmine would answer. Her grandmother ran her own law firm in DC.

"That's family," Grandma Hunt would say. "You need influences in all areas of life. I like that woman. You can tell she knows what she's doing just by looking at her."

At this moment, Principal Frederickson looked pretty severe.

"Jasmine, I need to discuss a serious matter with you," she said, looking Jasmine directly in the eyes. "It's regarding the missing ruby necklace."

"I know. It's just awful," Jasmine said.

"I was speaking with the librarian," the principal continued. "And she says that you spend a great deal of time in the reading room."

Jasmine nodded. "That's right." Why was Principal Frederickson bringing this up?

"And from what I've seen of the video footage so far, you spent quite a bit of time studying the ruby," the principal went on.

Jasmine suddenly got a sick feeling in the pit of her stomach.

"Wait one moment," said Mrs. Johnson angrily. "You don't think that Jasmine had anything to do with this, do you?"

"I didn't say that," Principal Frederickson said evenly. "I am just curious, that's all. Perhaps Jasmine saw or heard something that might help us."

"But I haven't been in the library for days," Jasmine protested, her voice rising with nervousness. "I just sketch it sometimes, that's all. I didn't notice anything about the theft. I was home on Friday night, and we went to a quiz bowl competition on Saturday. Ms. Keatley was with us."

"And your team did a very good job there," Principal Frederickson said. "We're not certain, but it appears that the necklace was stolen between nine a.m. and one p.m. last Saturday. If that is true, then you couldn't have *stolen* the necklace."

She emphasized the word "stolen," and Jasmine understood the implication: that maybe she still had something to do with the theft. Mrs. Johnson understood it, too, and she didn't like it one bit.

"If you have any more questions for Jasmine, I suggest you contact our lawyer," Jasmine's mom said, standing up. "I can't believe this, accusing a sixth-grade girl of being a jewel thief!"

"I am not accusing Jasmine of anything," the principal said, then raised her eyebrows. "And if by your 'lawyer' you mean Rose Hunt, then please say hello to your mother for me. We are old friends."

Mrs. Johnson relaxed a little bit. "So why are we here?"

Principal Frederickson looked at Jasmine. "I just wanted to see if Jasmine could help us in some way. But that's obviously not the case."

When they left the principal's office, Jasmine's mom gave her a hug. "That was a little scary!" she said. "I've never known Principal Frederickson to be so accusatory."

Jasmine made an anxious face.

Then the bell rang. "You'd better get back to class," her mom said. "Don't worry about this, Jasmine. I'm going to call Grandma when I get home."

"Thanks, Mom," Jasmine said, feeling only slightly relieved.

It wasn't easy for Jasmine to concentrate as the morning went on. She was glad when it became time for lunch and she could finally confide in her friends.

"So, Jazz, why'd you leave Biology?" Lili asked as they all sat down with their trays of salad and grilled chicken. "You missed a fascinating film. *Not!*"

"You guys won't believe what happened," Jasmine grumbled. She told them the whole story of her trip to the principal's office.

"That is ridiculous!" Erin fumed. "How could Principal Frederickson think you had anything to do with this?"

"Keep your voice down, please," Jasmine said, looking around. "I don't want other people to know about this." She took a deep breath. "She said there's a lot of video footage of me in the reading room, looking at the ruby."

"I guess that does seem sort of suspicious," Erin admitted reluctantly.

"Well, I can kind of see where Principal Frederickson is coming from," said Willow diplomatically. "I mean, you do spend a lot of time there. Maybe you did notice something strange, and you just can't remember?"

Jasmine shook her head. "Honestly, I don't. And besides, Principal Frederickson says they think it took place on Saturday, when we were at the Franklin quiz bowl. So how could I notice something if I wasn't even there?"

"Well, it's obvious that Principal Frederickson thinks you're a suspect of some kind," Lili said sympathetically. "That is so not fair!"

Then Erin grinned, and an excited look crossed her face. "I know how we can clear your name. We should find the real thieves ourselves!"

Chapter Five

Lili looked skeptical. "Quiz bowl stars? Check. Generally awesome people? Check. Detectives? I don't think so!"

"Come on," Erin pleaded. "We're smart, we make a great team, and Jazz needs us!"

For the first time since talking to Principal Frederickson, Jasmine felt the tight knot in her stomach begin to unravel. Her face brightened. "We could prove I'm innocent!"

"Lili's right," Willow said. "We're definitely not detectives or anything. But it wouldn't hurt to check things out or ask a couple of questions. We may find something the police missed. After all, who knows this school or the ruby better than us?"

"I'd do anything to help Jazz out!" Lili said. "I'm in!"

As the bell rang, Jasmine thanked everyone. "I'm so lucky to have friends like you."

They all picked up their trays. "We can talk more later," Willow said before they left for their afternoon classes.

But the girls had a busy week ahead, starting with a quiz bowl practice after school that day. Ms. Keatley seemed more flustered than usual. She was wearing a teal oversized knit tunic with black leggings, and her long blond hair was sticking up in spots. The Jewels knew it meant she had been running her fingers through it all day, a sure sign she was stressed.

"Composer Ludwig van Beethoven composed how many symphonies for orchestra?" she asked.

Lili raised her hand. "Nine."

"I'm sorry, Lili, that is wrong. The correct answer is . . ." she shuffled through the papers on her desk, then looked up sheepishly. "Nine. Oh dear. I'm sorry! This business about the ruby is just starting to really hit me, and I'm distracted. To think something like that could happen here!"

Erin gently nudged Willow in the side and looked at her with raised eyebrows. It was the perfect chance to ask some questions!

"It's terrible," Willow agreed. "But there's something I don't understand. Isn't there a video recorder in the library? Wouldn't whoever took the ruby be caught on tape?"

Ms. Keatley sighed. "You would think so. But the video camera went dead between the hours of nine a.m. and one p.m. It helps to narrow down when the ruby was stolen, but that's about it."

"Hmmmm." Lili looked thoughtful. "Must have been a pretty high-tech thief to know how to disable the camera."

Ms. Keatley glanced at the clock on the wall. "Enough about the ruby! I'm sorry I got us off on this tangent. Let's get back to practicing." She picked up a flash card from her desk.

"This German princess was named Sophie before becoming empress of Russia in 1762."

"Catherine the Great," Erin answered.

Ms. Keatley continued to ask questions of the girls, taking notes on areas they had trouble with.

"Great job!" she commended them after the practice hour was up. "It looks like you're in great shape for the next quiz bowl in two weeks, where I think you'll be matched with the Rivals for the first time. Of course, we'll get in some more practices before then, and the Hallytown Harvest Festival Think Out is this Sunday."

"Don't worry," Willow said. "We'll be ready for them."

Between Willow's soccer practice, Erin's guitar lessons, and Lili's Japanese tutoring, it wasn't easy for the girls to do any detective work. Thursday night, Erin impatiently texted her friends.

When r we going 2 start investigating?

We can talk Saturday at the museum, Willow typed back.

Cool with me! replied Lili.

Thx guys! Jasmine added.

On Saturday morning, the girls all met at the Metrorail train station at 8:30. Erin was yawning, Lili was snapping photos of fashionable people passing by, Jasmine was studying a guidebook, and Willow was sipping a yogurt smoothie.

"I hope Ms. Keatley's not late," Jasmine said worriedly, looking up from her book for their advisor. "The train will be here any minute."

But Ms. Keatley came running up just in time. "Sorry, girls!" she said, catching her breath. "My cat, Max, decided to attack the coffee machine this morning, and I had a big mess to clean up. I hope we haven't missed the train."

"No, we've still got five minutes," Willow reported.

The teacher relaxed. "That's good. I find that taking the train is so much nicer than dealing with all the traffic and parking. So, is everyone excited for our trip?"

"I've been thinking about where we should go," Jasmine said. "There's a lot of ground to cover. This guidebook says that the museum holds more than fifty thousand aircraft and spacecraft."

"You shouldn't have said that," Erin teased. "Willow will make you memorize them all."

"Hey!" Willow protested.

Jasmine made a face. She didn't think that was funny, either. Mostly because it was probably true! "So anyway, I thought we could narrow it down to some of the space exhibits. See? There's Space Race and Exploring the Universe . . ."

She held out the guidebook for her friends to see.

"Cool," Erin said. "And they're right next to the food court."

The train pulled into the station with a rush of wind. They quickly boarded and took their seats.

The girls were eager to talk about the ruby, so they were grateful when Ms. Keatley put in her earbuds to listen to classical music. Erin and Lili leaned over the backs of Willow's and Jasmine's seats so they could talk.

"All right," Erin said. "So what's the plan?"

Willow held up her smartphone, and Jasmine took out a notebook.

"Well, I was thinking . . ." they both said at the same time, and then they laughed.

"Figures you both have plans," Erin said. "Whaddya got?"

"Well, I just made some notes about what we know," Willow said. "Just the facts. We know the ruby was stolen between nine and one. And we know the thief was smart enough to disable the video camera."

"I had that, too," Jasmine interjected. "And then I made some notes about what we should do next. Like maybe we should take a good look at the library reading room. See if we find any clues."

"Exactly! We need to look for clues," Erin said. "I've always wanted an excuse to get one of those big magnifying glasses."

Willow flipped through her screen, looking at her schedule. "What about lunch on Monday? If anyone asks, we can say we're doing research on a paper or something?"

Erin frowned. "Do we really have to miss lunch?"

"I'll bring some extra cucumber sushi," Lili offered. "You can eat that real fast."

"Mmm, sushi," Erin said with a nod.

With the plan set, the girls settled back to enjoy the train ride. Within thirty minutes, the tree-lined suburbs of Hallytown gave way to the National Mall in Washington, DC, as the train slid underground. After they exited Union Station, Ms. Keatley led the way toward the Mall.

"This place is awesome," Erin said as they walked along the pathways of the grassy green promenade. "It's got all the best of the city in one place. There's the Lincoln Memorial on one end, the Capitol Building on the other, and tons of museums in between."

"And don't forget the Washington Monument," Jasmine added. "Eighty-one thousand tons of marble, granite, and . . . some other blue stone." She frowned. "I should know that."

"It's blue gneiss," Ms. Keatley said, and the girls looked at one another.

"One of these days, I hope I have an encyclopedia for a brain like you do," Erin told her.

The teacher smiled, pleased. "Oh, I just read a lot, that's all," she said.

Part of the Smithsonian Institution, the National Air and Space Museum sat in the center of the National Mall. From the front, the modern-looking building was a tower of steel and glass flanked by two even taller marble buildings. Lili stopped in front of the sculpture at the foot of the main stairs. It was a gleaming, gold-colored, stainless steel spire that came to a sharp point at the top. Circling the point was a cluster of starbursts made from thin rods.

"I soooo heart this!" she said, gazing up at the top. "Wouldn't it make an amazing hat?"

"It's called *Ad Astra*, which means 'to the stars,' " Jasmine said, reading from the guidebook.

Inside, the girls were greeted by another amazing sight: the Apollo 11 command module. They walked around the cone-shaped spacecraft, trying to gaze inside the glass windows.

"I can't believe they fit three astronauts in there," Willow said, reading the information plaque by the display.

"At least it's bigger than my bedroom," Erin joked.

"We should head to the Space Race exhibit," Jasmine suggested. "It's just down the hall."

"There sure is a lot of science in here," Erin remarked as they walked through the crowded halls. "Maybe next time we could go to the National Museum of American History. You get to learn about actual people there, not just boring machines."

"Astronauts are people," Ms. Keatley pointed out. "And there's tons of history in the Space Race exhibit. It tells the story of how the United States and the Soviet Union both tried to become the first nation to land a human on the moon."

"I know," Erin said. "I guess I just like my history old, you know?"

They quickly reached the exhibit, and Jasmine immediately got out a notebook and started taking notes and pictures. She wanted to make sure that the next time Willow counted missed answers, they weren't science ones.

There was a lot to look at, from Skylab, one of the first US space stations, to a test model of the Hubble Space Telescope. Not to be outdone by Jasmine, Willow began taking notes, too.

"It says that the Hubble circles around the Earth every ninety-seven minutes, at a speed of five miles per second," she muttered as she wrote. "So that's twenty-nine thousand miles every trip. Impressive."

"There goes Willow. Showing off her math genius again," Erin teased.

While Willow and Jasmine took notes, Lili wandered around with wide eyes, fascinated by the design of the spacecraft and other equipment. Only Erin quickly grew bored. She stepped back into the hallway, drawn by the smells of fried food wafting from the food court. As she walked closer to the museum's restaurants, she heard a familiar French accent coming from the other side of the lunar module.

"This is not the best museum at all." It was definitely Isabel from the Rivals. Curious, Erin slowly made her way around the module until she got close enough to see them.

Erin recognized Ryan and Isabel. They were talking to the two other Rivals teammates: Veronica Manasas and Aaron Santiago. Veronica was shorter than the rest of them and wearing jeans and a baggy sweatshirt. Her black hair was pulled into a ponytail. Aaron looked pretty spiffy for a Saturday in a button-down shirt.

"We've got to think about every possibility," Ryan was saying. "We have to do this right."

"Let's check out the Space Race room," Veronica said. "It's right over there, and it's got some interesting stuff inside."

Erin quickly ran from the module and went to find her friends. She bumped into Willow first.

"You'll never believe who I just saw," she said, breathless.

Willow looked past her and saw the Rivals. "Seriously? What are they doing here?"

Ryan saw Willow looking at him, and at first he made a ducking move, like he didn't want to be seen. But then Willow waved and called, "Hey, Ryan!"

The Rivals all looked at one another, and Erin could have sworn they were nervous. They walked up to meet Willow and Erin, led by a reluctant Ryan. Willow made sure she got the first word in.

"So, what are you guys doing here?" she asked.

Ryan shrugged. "We're just, uh, brushing up on our science."

Behind him, Isabel looked angry. "That is ridiculous! We do not need to brush up on anything!" she protested, and Aaron nudged her.

"I guess we're doing that, too, then," Willow said carefully. "You know, keeping sharp for our next meet. Will we see you guys at the Think Out?"

The Think Out was a quiz bowl event at the Hallytown Harvest Festival. It was mostly for fun, a chance for local schools to show off.

"No," Ryan replied. "It doesn't count toward nationals or anything. Or didn't you know that?"

"We might be new to the circuit, but we can still read the schedule," Willow retorted, annoyed. "Anyway, it'll be fun."

"Plus they have corn dogs!" Erin chimed in.

Isabel made a face. "Let me guess. This is something you eat? A corn dog? It sounds disgusting."

"Oh yeah, well, so is . . ." Erin searched her mind for something French she could insult. ". . . French toast!"

"See you guys around," Ryan said with a smirk, and the Rivals hurried off.

Willow glared at Erin. "French toast? Seriously?"

Erin shrugged. "It was all I could think of. Who does she think she is, insulting corn dogs like that?"

Lili and Jasmine found them.

"So, should we head to the next exhibit?" Jasmine asked.

"First we should make sure the Rivals aren't there," Erin groaned.

Lili looked confused. "What do you mean?"

Willow explained their encounter, and Jasmine shook her head.

"It's like we can't get away from them." She sighed.

"Well, I guess it makes sense, since Atkinson Prep is right next to Hallytown," Willow pointed out. "And anyway, they said they're not going to the Think Out tomorrow."

"Yeah, they probably think it's beneath them or something," Erin said.

"Well, let's forget about the Rivals. I want to see the Explore the Universe exhibit," Jasmine suggested. "We should get Ms. Keatley. She's been staring at the space suits for, like, fifteen minutes."

"Can we stop in the food court first?" Erin asked. "Talking to snooty people always makes me hungry!"

Chapter Six

"Ready? Set? Go!" Delia Winters, the owner of Sweet Treats Bakery, yelled.

At a table covered with a red-and-white checkered tablecloth sat ten people. Each had an entire pie sitting in front of them, and everyone's hands were tied behind their backs. When Delia yelled "Go!" ten heads dove into their pies.

"Eli! Remember how to do it!" Lili yelled loudly.

Eli looked up from his pie and grinned. His face was already smeared with apple pie filling. He grabbed the foil pie plate with his teeth and turned it over on the table. The pie slid out, and Eli went to work, gobbling it up.

It was a beautiful fall Sunday and perfect weather for the Hallytown Harvest Festival. Main Street had been closed off to traffic and transformed with haystacks, pumpkins, and scarecrows. Booths were set up, and vendors were selling handmade crafts, baked goods, and other items. But the Jewels were all gathered around the main stage, where Lili's brother was participating in the pie-eating contest.

Out of nowhere, Willow started laughing. "This reminds me of a joke: What do you get if you divide the circumference of a jack-o'-lantern by its diameter? Pumpkin pi. Get it? Pi, the mathematical constant approximately equal to three-point-one-four?" She started cracking up.

Jasmine chuckled, but Erin pretended to look horrified. "We need to get you out more. And not to museums or quiz bowls! You need a day of no-brain-required fun."

"That's what this is!" Lili pointed to the stage as she began to chant, "E-li! E-li! E-li! E-li!" over and over again.

Willow joined her, jumping up and down and clapping. "You can do it, Eli!"

Then Eli stood up, pie filling dripping from his face. Delia hurried over to check his empty pie plate.

"The winner!" she yelled.

"Yes!" Lili cheered, giving Willow a high five. "Way to go, bro!"

"That was fun!" Jasmine said. "But messy. I hope they give Eli a wet wipe or something."

"I hope they clean that stage off before the Think Out," Willow added. "I don't want to go to hit the buzzer and end up with a handful of apple pie instead."

"Well, I do!" Erin said, with big eyes.

"About the Think Out." Jasmine frowned. "Do we really have to wear these?" She pointed to her shirt.

Each of the girls wore a black T-shirt, bedazzled with the words "Jewels Rule!" in red and white rhinestones and decorated with glitter swirls.

"They are corny chic," Lili explained. "Like ugly Christmas sweaters. Cool people will get the irony. Plus, I spent all night making them!"

"You know how I feel about fake gemstones," Jasmine complained.

"But the slogan is awesome," Erin pointed out.

"That's because you thought of it," Jasmine reminded her.

"Yeah, but anyway, I kind of like them," Erin said. "They're super sparkly."

"They definitely show off our team spirit," Willow said encouragingly. "And they're perfect for the Think Out today. We don't have to make them the official team uniform if we all don't agree to it."

"That's fair," Jasmine said. "But I don't think I'll change my mind!"

After the remains of the pie-eating contest were cleaned up, the mayor of Hallytown, Barbara Gilmore, waited on the side of the stage. Next to her stood a confident-looking teenage girl with long black hair. She wore a red gown with a puffy skirt and a sash that said "Miss Hallytown."

"Wow, that's a great dress," Lili said admiringly. "She looks like a princess."

"Yeah, and she acts like one, too."

The girls turned to see Veronica Manasas of the Rivals standing behind them. She wore jeans and a sweatshirt, just like she had at the museum. Her black hair was held back with a headband, although a few wisps had escaped and were hanging on her forehead.

Erin looked from Veronica to Miss Hallytown. "No way. Is that your sister?"

Veronica sighed and rolled her eyes. "Yes, that is the amazing Amelia," she said sarcastically.

A short woman with perfectly styled wavy hair breezed by the girls and stopped when she saw Veronica.

"Don't look so miserable, sweetie," she said, clicking her tongue. "You should be happy for your sister. And pay attention. You could be Miss Hallytown one day, too!"

Then she hurried off and began fussing over Amelia.

"Was that your mom?" Willow asked.

Veronica nodded. "Oh yes," she said glumly.

"Let me guess," Erin said. "Your mom thinks your older sister is perfect, and doesn't let you forget it, right?"

"Yeah," Veronica said. "How did you —"

"I know, 'cause I've got one, too," Erin explained. "If I hear one more time 'Mary Ellen did this' or 'Mary Ellen did that,' I'm going to scream!"

Veronica relaxed a bit. "Science is my life. You think my parents would give me some credit. Scientists cure disease and help change the way the world works. But oh no, my beauty queen sister is the best thing since nuclear fission."

The audience applauded as the mayor and Amelia got onstage to crown the new Miss Hallytown. When the ceremony ended, a crew began to set the stage for the Think Out.

"Good luck, guys," Veronica said. She smiled at Erin, then walked off to find her family.

Jasmine turned to her friends. "Is it possible? One of the Rivals is actually nice?"

"Why not?" Willow asked. "They can't all be as bad as Isabel."

"I sure hope not," Erin said.

Willow glanced up at the stage. "Looks like it's time for our match."

"No pressure, Jewels!" Lili said. "Remember, this quiz bowl is for fun only. The win won't count toward nationals."

Willow made a face. "But we still want to do as well as we can," she pointed out. "After all, this is Martha Washington's first year in the Think Out. We want to make a name for ourselves."

Lili only laughed at Willow's seriousness. "Relax! We're going to be awesome. But first we need some brain food. Where is that corn dog truck?"

Erin tilted her nose in the air and sneered. "You mean ze dog of ze corn? Such a thing will not pass zese perfect lips," she said in a really bad French accent. The girls doubled over in laughter.

"I hate to say it, but I agree with Isabel on that one," Willow said. "I brought my own brain food." She dug into her backpack and came out with a plastic bag. "Peanut butter and whole-grain crackers, anyone?"

The girls eagerly shared Willow's snack.

"This is much better than that tin of sardines you tried to get us to eat before that one practice," Jasmine told Willow. "They were gross!"

"Lili and I wouldn't even try them," Erin added. "And you could only eat one yourself, Willow, remember?"

Willow shuddered, thinking of those little salty fish. "I read they were a super brain food. Hey, at least I gave it a shot!"

"You threw them into the garbage can, and it was a Saturday," Jasmine reminded her. "When Ms. Keatley went into her classroom on Monday, she thought something had crawled under her desk and died!"

The girls broke into peals of laughter.

"Ms. Keatley was ready to call poison control," Lili giggled.

"Are you talking about the sardine incident again?" Ms. Keatley asked as she joined the group. "I swear, on a humid day I can still smell them sometimes."

Willow cringed.

"No worries." Ms. Keatley smiled. "I think it's great that for a team that hasn't been together that long, we already have a history. Is everyone ready for the Think Out?" The girls nodded. "Remember how this is going to work: Two teams will compete against each other in a miniround. These are high-speed rounds, with no bonus questions. The winning team moves on, and the losing team is out of the competition. It will continue until only one team is left."

"So that means we'll have to win all six rounds to be the champions." Jasmine looked worried.

Willow gave a confident grin. "We can do this!"

The Jewels took to the stage and lined up behind their buzzers. Lili went over to Jasmine and tugged off her sweater, revealing the glittery "Jewels" shirt Lili had made. Jasmine sighed.

For this special match, Mayor Gilmore was acting as the Think Out moderator. She welcomed the Jewels and their opponents from Fox Farm Middle School.

As Mayor Gilmore began to read the first question, Jasmine felt like her stomach was in knots. The team's bedazzled T-shirts weren't the only thing making her nervous. She didn't want the science questions to be the Jewels' downfall. She had to concentrate!

"After which scientist is the world's first space-based optical telescope named?" she asked.

Jasmine pressed the buzzer in a flash.

"Martha Washington," Mayor Gilmore acknowledged.

"Edwin P. Hubble," she answered confidently.

"That is correct," the mayor replied.

Willow flashed a smile at Jasmine along with a thumbs-up. Their trip to the National Air and Space Museum was already paying off!

The first round seemed like a blur as the questions kept coming at a fast pace. Fox Farm earned a few points, but the Jewels were the first team to answer four questions correctly! Next they faced North River Middle School.

"Who was the first human in space?"

The mayor called on North River.

"Alan Shepard?" a boy answered.

"Incorrect. Martha Washington?"

"Yuri Gagarin?" Erin answered, her face turning red.

"Correct!"

Erin let out a big exhale. She might have been bored by the Space Race exhibit, but at least she had remembered some stuff.

The Jewels were on fire. They were hitting their buzzers so often that Lili had started to blow on her hands — the buzzer was getting hot!

"What is the decimal for one-sixteenth?"

Willow buzzed in. "Zero-point-zero-six-two-five."

"Which artist painted *The Scream*?"

"Edvard Munch!" Lili answered.

Team after team left the stage as the Jewels captivated the crowd with their rapid-fire answers.

After winning five matches, they faced their sixth and final team. If they got this one last question right, they'd be the Hallytown Harvest Festival Think Out Champions!

"Name the first US space station."

Jasmine's buzzer rang out. "That would be Skylab."

The mayor smiled. "Correct! The winner of this match, and of the entire Think Out, is the Martha Washington Jewels!"

The crowd cheered. Erin and Lili grabbed hands and started jumping up and down. Jasmine and Willow joined in, too.

"We did it!" Willow cried. Ms. Keatley ran up to them.

"Group hug!" Lili grabbed everyone together.

"Wonderful job, girls!" Ms. Keatley said. "You're more than ready to face the Rivals at next Saturday's competition."

Erin grinned. "I was *born* ready!"

Chapter Seven

The next morning, all of the Jewels were still flying high as they met outside the school.

"Everyone is buzzing about us!" Willow said proudly. "I heard all the other schools are betting we'll be the ones to end the Rivals' winning streak."

"They're smart to bet on us," Erin said. "We're so going to destroy those guys!"

Jasmine turned to Lili. "I'm sorry, but I think it's back to the drawing board for our uniforms," she said. "They're cool, but I just felt like too much of a show-off in that shirt. It was hard to concentrate!"

"No prob!" Lili said cheerfully. "I'll come up with something even cooler for our next match."

They joined the throngs of girls walking into the school.

"So the plan is on, right?" Erin asked in a loud whisper. "We're going to investigate the library for clues? I bought a big magnifying glass last night after the Harvest Festival."

"And I brought the cucumber sushi," Lili said.

Willow nodded. "We're on."

The morning seemed to go by so slowly. When lunchtime finally came, the girls quickly ate and then headed through the busy hallways to the library.

In the main room, several students were sitting at the round tables, studying. Police tape still blocked the entrance to the reading room through the back wall.

"Let's act casual, like we're looking for books," Willow suggested in a whisper. "Then we'll make our way over there."

Jasmine looked worried. "Oh, I hope Mrs. Potter doesn't notice," she said, nodding toward the librarian's desk. The gray-haired woman was busy typing something on a computer.

"Looking around isn't a crime," Erin pointed out. "Come on, let's go."

The girls slowly made their way to the back of the library, stopping to look at books on the shelves as they went. When they got to the reading room, they peered through the tape. In the center of the room stood the ruby's glass display case, but it was bare.

"I've never seen that case empty," Jasmine said wistfully. "It's so strange."

Her eyes roamed around the small room, searching for any sign of something out of place. With the exception of the ruby being gone, everything looked exactly the same.

"It seems pretty normal," Jasmine said, shaking her head.

Erin was holding a big magnifying glass up to her eye. "Yeah, everything's just kind of blurry," she said.

Jasmine glanced around the library. Nobody seemed to be paying attention to them, but she was still nervous. Mrs. Potter could notice them snooping around at any minute, and Erin's magnifying glass was the opposite of subtle.

"Come on, let's go," she urged her friends. "There are obviously no leads here."

She turned to leave when something shiny caught her eye.

"Look at that!" She pointed to a glittering object on the library's dark wood floor, just inside the door to the reading room.

"A clue!" Erin exclaimed. "I think I can reach it."

She leaned over and stretched her arm under the yellow tape, carefully scooping up the object on the floor. "Got it!"

Erin opened her hand as the other girls gathered around. Inside lay a circular silver pin with a bright blue stone in the center. The words "Brain Brawl Champions" were inscribed around the edge.

"Brain Brawl — that's the name of the eastern regional quiz bowl championship tournament," Willow said.

"Martha Washington hasn't had a team in a long time, let alone won a championship," Jasmine commented.

"So someone from a different quiz bowl team must have dropped it!" Lili began to get excited. "Do you know what that means?"

"It means that someone from another school must have been in the library," Willow said. "They could be our thief!"

"We can check the visitors' book in the front office to see who has signed in recently. I know the library is open Saturday for the math study group, so anyone could have gotten in," Erin said. She looked at her watch. "Lunch is almost over, though. We can go right after school."

"Sounds good to me," Jasmine said. "Now let's get out of here."

Erin handed her the pin. "You spotted it. You should keep it."

Jasmine slipped the pin into the front pocket of her bag. "I'll keep it safe," she promised.

When the last bell rang, the girls met in the hallway in front of the main office.

"What do we do, just march in and demand to see the book?" Lili asked.

"It's sitting right on the counter," Erin responded. "I don't think it's classified information. But you guys can distract Ms. Ortiz while I look, just so she's not suspicious."

They walked toward the entrance of the school and turned into the front office. Ms. Ortiz, a young woman with long, curly hair, greeted them with a smile.

"Hi there, girls! Willow, how's your mother?" she asked. "I've been meaning to sign up for the next round of yoga classes at the community center, but I hurt my knee playing Frisbee this past weekend. Wasn't the weather beautiful? Do you know if there are any spots left in the class?" Before Willow could answer, Ms. Ortiz went right on talking. "If my knee isn't better, maybe I'll try the knitting class. I've heard it can be very relaxing."

Erin stifled a laugh as Ms. Ortiz kept chatting to Willow. She shot a glance at Lili and Jasmine. They should have figured the talkative secretary would be easy to distract. Erin leafed through the pages of the visitors' book, paying careful attention to the day of and days leading up to the theft.

A quick scan showed no unusual visitors — and not anyone from another school.

"Tell your mom I tried her banana bread recipe." Ms. Ortiz was still talking when Erin shut the book. "It was delicious! So, can I help you girls with anything?"

Willow shook her head. "We just wanted to stop by and say hi."

Ms. Ortiz beamed. "Isn't that nice? Have a great afternoon. Come by anytime!"

In the hallway, the girls looked at Erin quizzically.

"Nothing," she said. "But I guess a thief wouldn't sign in!"

"So, we're back at square one," Willow said. "I wonder why the pin doesn't have a year on it. That could tell us which team won it."

"I think I know a way," Jasmine said. Deep in thought, she took the pin out of her bag and examined it.

"This is an aquamarine," she finally said. "Lili, can I borrow your phone?"

Lili handed it over reluctantly. Students were not supposed to use cell phones at school unless it was an emergency. Jasmine used the web browser to do a search. "Aha!" she cried. "It's just what I thought. Each year the Brain Brawl championship pins have a different gemstone on them. If we can find out which year had the aquamarine, we can find out which quiz bowl team the pin belongs to." She ran her fingertip along the touch screen as she searched for the answer. "The aquamarine was the gem for . . ." Her eyes continued to scan the screen. ". . . the fifth-grade winners of last year's tournament. And the winners of last year's Brain Brawl were . . . the Atkinson Prep Rivals!"

"The Rivals!" Erin gasped. "I should have guessed!"

"So, last year's fifth-grade team would be this year's sixth-grade team," Willow said thoughtfully. "So this pin belongs to Ryan, Isabel, Veronica, or Aaron."

"Not Isabel," Jasmine reminded her. "She wasn't on the team last year."

"The Rivals were late to the Franklin quiz bowl," Lili pointed out.

"Well, they had a late *slot*." Her eyes widened. "They could have been right here stealing the necklace that morning!"

"Wait a sec," Willow said. "A pin and not being on time to the quiz bowl don't mean anything. We need more proof. If they weren't at the quiz bowl that morning, they could have been somewhere else. We need to find out what each one of them was doing on Saturday morning."

Erin frowned. "I can't imagine Veronica is a thief."

"We need to find out for sure," Willow said, then thought for a moment. "An easy way to start is by checking each of the Rivals' Chatter statuses for two Saturdays ago."

Willow pulled out her phone and pressed the screen. "Let's see," she said. "Ryan did a sign-in on Saturday at eleven a.m. from the movie theater. It says he was there with Aaron, catching a matinee."

Willow continued to read from her phone. "Isabel signed in at the mall around eleven a.m. She even posted a photo of a pair of boots she was trying on at Shoe Crazy. Veronica signed in from the Marian Koshland Science Museum at about the same time. It says she was enjoying the infectious disease exhibit."

Lili stuck her tongue out. "Barf!"

"So they all have alibis, then?" Jasmine seemed disappointed.

"Wait!" Lili said. She grabbed her phone back from Jasmine and logged in to her Chatter account. "I'm using my cell phone, right? There are two ways I can use it. If I use Chatter's sign-in feature, it automatically picks up my location from my phone. But I can bypass it and choose to sign myself in from anywhere. See?"

She held up her phone. Her Chatter status said, "Lili Higashida is at the National Gallery of Art."

"But I'm not!" Lili said. "I'm right here at Martha Washington School."

"So the Rivals could have faked their alibis?" Willow asked.

"Yes." Lili nodded. "And if they did, then they could be the jewel thieves!"

Chapter Eight

Jasmine frowned. "That would be proof, all right. But how are *we* going to prove that they faked their alibis?"

"Well, we don't have to worry about Isabel, because we know the pin wasn't hers," Willow said thoughtfully. "So that leaves Ryan, Aaron, and Veronica."

"Eli knows Ryan and Aaron," Lili piped up. "Maybe he could ask them questions about the movie they saw. You know, to be sure they actually saw it."

Willow nodded. She turned to Jasmine. "Jazz, do you think we could go to the science museum after school this week?"

"I'll ask my mom," Jasmine said. "Maybe she can take us."

"Why don't Lili and I hit the mall?" Erin suggested. "If we find out that Isabel was lying, too, then it makes our case stronger, right?"

"Yay! The mall!" Lili cheered.

Willow smiled. "So I guess we have a plan."

"This is so exciting!" Erin said. "It's like we're real detectives."

"It's totally fun," Lili agreed. "Hey, what do detectives wear? Maybe we need some cool hats or something."

Jasmine looked anxious. "I don't know. It doesn't feel fun. I mean, I want to prove I'm innocent, but I don't want to get in any more trouble."

"We're not doing anything wrong," Willow assured her. Her brown eyes were sparkling, and it was clear that she was excited about the challenge. "And if we're right about the Rivals, we'll be heroes!"

Lili and Erin were the first to do their part. The next day, Erin's dad took them to the mall after school.

"I hope you girls don't plan to be here for hours," Mr. Fischer said, looking around at the brightly lit shops apprehensively.

"We'll be fast, Dad," Erin promised. "We just need to go check something out at Shoe Crazy."

"Shoe Crazy? Is that actually the name of a store?" he asked, shaking his head. "Unbelievable."

There was a bench right outside the Shoe Crazy shop, so Erin's dad settled in and read a book while Lili and Erin went inside.

"Ooh, look!" Lili said, darting toward a pair of sparkly silver heels.

"Where would you even wear those?" Erin asked.

"Anywhere!" Lili said confidently. She picked one up. "I wonder if they have them in my size."

"We're not here to shop, remember?" Erin said. "Come on, give me your phone. I don't have a Chatter account on mine."

Lili handed over her bright purple phone, and Erin found the photo that Isabel had posted of the boots. She marched up to the bored-looking teenage salesgirl at the front of the store. The girl's long bangs almost covered her sleepy eyes, and she leaned against the counter, covering her mouth as she yawned.

"Excuse me. Do you have these boots?" Erin asked, holding the phone up to show her the picture.

The girl rolled her eyes and twirled her long hair around one finger. "Those are, like, so last month."

"But are they still on the shelves?" Erin asked. "Like, did you have any in stock a couple Saturdays ago?"

The girl sighed. "No. They've been totally sold out since, like, forever."

"So she's lying!" Lili cried out.

"Whatever," the salesgirl said. "I am not."

"I don't mean *you*, I mean — oh, you know what I mean," Lili said, turning to Erin.

Erin nodded. "Isabel must have taken a photo of some boots she bought here last month! So I would say her alibi is definitely busted."

On Wednesday after school, Mrs. Johnson took Jasmine and Willow to the Marian Koshland Science Museum.

"So you have a report due on infectious diseases?" Jasmine's mom said as they entered the museum. "That sounds . . . um . . . interesting."

"Thanks for bringing us," Jasmine told her mom. "This is really going to help with our reports."

"If you don't mind, I think I'll head to the Lights at Night exhibit," Mrs. Johnson said. "Call my cell if you need me."

Jasmine and Willow headed to the Infectious Diseases area.

"Your mom seems kind of grossed out," Willow remarked.

"I don't blame her," Jasmine said. "It does sound pretty gross."

But the gallery was actually kind of cool, with brightly lit interactive photo and video panels. You could press a button and watch a video on a number of topics, from vaccines to viruses.

"So what are we looking for, exactly?" Jasmine wondered.

"I'm not sure," Willow admitted. "Let me check Veronica's Chatter page again and see if there's something there that can help."

Willow took out her phone, and after a few seconds, she frowned.

"That's weird. I can't get a signal," she said.

"Let me try," Jasmine suggested, but she didn't have any luck, either.

"Hmm," Willow said thoughtfully. She walked over to the nearest museum guide, an older man in a blue jacket. "Excuse me, but I can't seem to get a cell phone signal."

"I've never been able to get one inside the building," the guide informed her. "I always have to walk outside to use mine."

Willow turned to Jasmine. "So Veronica couldn't have posted her status from the exhibit!"

"Unless she went outside to do it," Jasmine pointed out.

"That seems like a lot of trouble," Willow said. "Anyway, it's the best proof we have."

After the girls studied the exhibit and Veronica's Chatter post, the missing cell phone signal was the only clue they could come up with. But the next day, Eli finally approached Ryan and Aaron at their school.

At first, Eli had refused when Lili asked for his help.

"What do you want me to do, grill them like some police detective?" Eli had asked. "That's weird."

"You don't have to do that," Lili replied. "Maybe just ask them some questions about the movie they posted about, to see if they really saw it."

"If they are master jewel thieves, then they probably read the movie review so they know what happens," Eli pointed out.

"But movie reviews don't tell you everything," Lili said. She reached into her backpack. "Here's ten bucks. Go see the movie and then talk to Ryan and Aaron about it."

Eli thought for a moment. "What movie is it?" he asked.

"*Curse of the Black Tiger*," Lili replied.

Eli had been wanting to see that one for a while; he loved ninja movies.

"Ten more bucks," Eli said. "I want to bring Zane."

Lili scowled. "You want me to pay for your best friend, too? That's . . . bribery!"

"No, actually, it's extortion," Eli told her. "But that's the deal. Besides, I might need Zane's help."

"Fine," Lili said reluctantly, handing over another ten-dollar bill with a sigh. "This is going to make a big dent in my glitter fund."

*   *   *

Eli and Zane saw the movie. And the next day, they positioned themselves next to Ryan and Aaron in the school courtyard.

"Man, *Curse of the Black Tiger* was awesome," Eli said loudly to Zane. Then he turned to the sixth graders. "Did you guys see it?"

Ryan and Aaron looked at each other for a moment.

"Yeah," Ryan said. "It was definitely awesome, all right."

"How about that twist ending?" Eli asked.

"Yeah, I wasn't expecting that," Zane agreed, nodding his head.

Eli looked directly at Ryan. "Did you guys see that coming?"

"Well, yeah, it was sort of obvious," Ryan said smugly. "Right, Aaron?"

Aaron looked uncomfortable. "Um, yeah. Sure."

Eli held back a smile. His little sister had been right! There was no twist ending in the movie at all. Ryan and Aaron were lying. But why? Because they were jewel thieves, like Lili said? It seemed kind of hard to believe.

"Cool. Later, dudes," Eli said, and then he motioned for Zane to walk away.

"So why did we do that, again?" Zane asked him.

"I told you, if you wanted the free ticket, no questions asked," Eli reminded him.

73

Friday at lunch, Lili told the Jewels what Eli had learned.

"So Ryan and Aaron were *definitely* lying," she said.

"Just like Isabel," Erin added.

"And most likely Veronica," said Jasmine.

Willow was frantically typing into her laptop. "I'm adding that to our report. After school we go see Principal Frederickson, right?"

The girls looked at one another nervously. "Are you sure we have enough proof?" Erin asked.

"We know they were at the scene of the crime. We know that they lied about where they were. That seems like pretty good proof to me," Willow said.

When the final bell rang, the girls met in the sixth-grade hall and then went to Principal Frederickson's office.

"How lovely to see you again, girls," said Ms. Ortiz. "Can I help you with something, or are you just here to chat?"

"We'd like to see Principal Frederickson," Willow said. "If she's not busy."

"Let me check," the secretary said. She picked up the phone and dialed. "The Jewels team is here to see you. Okay, then." Ms. Ortiz smiled. "Go right in."

The girls entered the principal's office and sat down in front of her desk.

"Congratulations on winning the Think Out. I'm very pleased to see you all doing so well in Martha Washington's first year back on the circuit," the principal said with a rare smile.

"Thank you, ma'am," Willow replied anxiously.

"So what brings you ladies here today?" Principal Frederickson asked.

Erin, Jasmine, and Lili all looked at Willow. She took a breath and handed the principal their report.

"We think that the Atkinson Prep academic team stole the Martha Washington ruby," she said.

Normally the principal's face wore the same calm expression every day, but Jasmine was sure she noticed a flicker of surprise in her eyes, though it quickly faded. She raised an eyebrow.

"That is a very serious accusation," she said.

"But we have evidence," Willow countered. "They all lied about their alibis from nine to one on the Saturday when the ruby was stolen."

"And one of them dropped this in the library," Jasmine added, placing the championship pin on the table.

The principal picked it up and examined it. "I see," she said. "This is very interesting." Then she began to read Willow's report, and her eyes got that look again. Jasmine got the feeling that the Jewels had found out something important, and Principal Frederickson knew it.

"Are you going to tell the police?" Erin asked.

Principal Frederickson put down the report. "I'm not sure if this evidence warrants police involvement," she replied crisply. "Martha Washington and Atkinson Prep have a long history together. Out of courtesy, I should bring this to Arthur Atkinson's attention first."

The girls looked at one another, and Willow gave a nod.

"Okay," Willow said. "Um, thanks for listening to us."

The principal stood up, and her manner was all business once more. "Enjoy your weekend," she said curtly, and it was clear she wanted them to leave.

Back in the hallway, the girls began to talk all at once.

"She's not going to the police!" Erin said.

"But at least she believed us," Lili pointed out.

"Did she?" Jasmine asked thoughtfully. "I mean, I thought she did, but then why isn't she going to the police?"

"She knows the best thing to do," Willow argued. "It's in her hands now. I'm sure she'll take care of it. She trusts us. Principal Frederickson is the one who brought the team together, after all."

Jasmine frowned. "I hope you're right. I hope *we're* right, and the Rivals have that ruby."

That night, the stolen ruby haunted Jasmine's dreams. Principal Frederickson was pointing at her, and her finger grew longer and longer.

"*You* did it!" the principal accused.

For once, Jasmine was glad to wake up early on a Saturday. She was digging into a bowl of granola at the kitchen table when her cell phone rang.

It was Willow. "Jazz. Turn on News Twelve right now."

Puzzled, Jasmine raced to the living room and switched on the TV, turning to the local news channel. A tall man wearing a blue pinstripe suit was talking into the camera. Underneath him on the screen it said, "Arthur Atkinson, Director of Atkinson Preparatory School."

"So as you can see, I have allowed the police to search every inch of the school, and no ruby was found," he was saying. "Right now, police are searching the homes of our sixth-grade academic team members, and I assure you that they won't find anything there, either. We have absolutely nothing to hide!"

"Mr. Atkinson, what led to these accusations?" the reporter asked.

"From what I have learned, these *false* accusations were made by a competing sixth-grade academic team, the Martha Washington Jewels," he said, and Jasmine gasped. Mr. Atkinson continued. "They're obviously trying to discredit our team so we'll be disqualified from future competitions. Outrageous!"

Chapter Nine

"Did you hear that?" Willow asked. "He says he called the police himself after Principal Frederickson talked to him."

"The shadow of thievery will not stain our school's reputation!" Atkinson was yelling into the camera, and Jasmine turned off the TV. It was too hard to watch.

"I can't believe he called us out . . . on TV," she groaned. "This is so embarrassing!"

"And don't forget," Willow said. "The competition today is being hosted by Atkinson Prep."

Jasmine groaned again. "Can this day get any worse?" She dumped her granola into the garbage. She had lost her appetite.

"Jasmine? Are you there?" Willow asked on the phone.

Jasmine felt like crying. This was even worse than her nightmare!

"I'm here," she said in a sad voice. "Willow, what are we going to do?"

"Let's meet at school an hour before we're supposed to leave for the quiz bowl so we can all talk about this," Willow suggested. "I'll let Erin and Lili know."

When Jasmine walked into Ms. Keatley's classroom later that morning, Willow was there waiting for her. They looked at each other and shook their heads sadly.

"I feel like it's all my fault," Willow said. "I'm the one who wanted to tell Principal Frederickson."

Just then, Erin burst into the room, and she looked angry.

"Your fault?" she asked. "No way! What kind of an adult goes on the news to bad-mouth sixth-grade kids? What a creep!"

She collapsed into a chair, holding her phone.

"I've been getting texts all morning," Erin complained. "Frankie, one of my friends from the Colonial quiz bowl team, said he thought we were supposed to be the good guys! Now everyone thinks we're jerks."

Willow frowned. "I haven't checked my Chatter page yet." She pulled out her phone. Her frown deepened as she read the messages.

"Here's a post from our 'friend'" — Willow said the word sarcastically — "Isabel. It says, 'Who's the cheater now?'"

Lili moped in, her shoulders hunched over. There wasn't a dash of glitter to be seen anywhere on her outfit.

"Hey," she said in a quiet voice. "Worst day ever, or what?"

The rest of the Jewels exchanged worried glances. Lili could find the silver lining in anything, even when the cafeteria served meat loaf. Without even realizing it, they'd all been counting on her to cheer them up somehow.

"Yes." Erin nodded. "The. Worst. Day. Ever," she said, slowly emphasizing each word.

"My mom is furious," Willow said. "She's going to call Principal Frederickson first thing Monday morning."

Jasmine thought of her mother walking in right after she'd gotten off the phone with Willow that morning. Through her tears, Jasmine had barely been able to explain to her what had happened.

"My mom said maybe I shouldn't be on the quiz bowl team anymore," Jasmine admitted. "She said all this drama isn't healthy."

Lili nodded. "My mom was even talking about sending me to Atkinson with Eli!" She avoided looking at her friends' faces. "She said that maybe you guys aren't good influences. I told her the truth, and she seemed to believe me. But if anything else happens, I'm Atkinson bound."

Willow worried that her quiz bowl championship dreams were dying. But even worse was the thought of losing her friends.

"We've got to stick together," Willow said, "and get through today, no matter how tough it's going to be."

Lili shuddered. "I can't imagine standing in the Atkinson theater with everyone staring at us, judging."

"I know my team," Ms. Keatley said as she walked into the classroom. She was carrying a large bakery box. "And they are a good, honest team, and I'm proud to be their advisor. I'll tell that to anyone, any newscaster, anywhere." She placed the box down on her desk.

The girls raced to Ms. Keatley, nearly knocking her over as they embraced her.

"Whoa!" she said as she steadied herself. "Now, who wants a doughnut? They always cheer me up when I'm feeling down."

The girls opened the box. For the first time that day, Lili's face brightened. "Oh, pink with sprinkles — my favorite!" she said as she reached for one.

They all grabbed a doughnut, even Willow, who picked a chocolate-filled one.

"I want you to know that I spoke with Principal Frederickson this morning," Ms. Keatley said as the girls snacked. "She's very upset that Arthur Atkinson contacted the news media. It was her hope that things could be handled quietly. However, now that the search showed that the ruby is not at Atkinson or hidden at any of the Rivals' homes, she wants you to forget about the matter and concentrate on the quiz bowl instead. Although," she looked sympathetically at the girls, "we both understand if you would like to forfeit today's match. It's up to you."

Willow immediately shook her head. "If we don't show up, it will look like Arthur Atkinson was right about us. We weren't trying to blame the Rivals just so we could win competitions. We had good reason to think they might have stolen the ruby. And I'm still not convinced that they didn't!"

"You've got to let that go," Ms. Keatley gently reminded her. "But I admire your attitude. What do the rest of you think?"

"I have nothing to be ashamed about," Erin said defiantly. "I say we go. And when I see that Mr. Atkinson, boy, am I gonna give him a piece of my mind!"

Ms. Keatley shook her head. "You'll do nothing of the sort. Today is all about taking the high road, so you'll have to keep your temper in check. Promise?" Erin sighed, but nodded yes. "Lili? Jasmine?"

Lili and Jasmine glanced at each other.

"Everyone is going to be looking at us and talking about us!" Jasmine said fearfully. "It's going to be awful. But if Willow and Erin can do it, so can I."

Lili smiled. "What the heck, I'm in, too!"

* * *

On the drive to Atkinson Prep, their confidence began to leave them. Usually before a meet, they would test one another with flash cards. Today they were all too nervous to concentrate, even Willow. As Ms. Keatley drove her old Volvo station wagon through Atkinson's six-acre campus, the Jewels only became more intimidated.

The school's six buildings were spread out among an impressive parklike setting full of gardens and playing fields. The main building, made of red sandstone, resembled a medieval castle, complete with turrets. It stood three stories high, dominating the landscape.

Erin gulped. "I wonder if they have a dungeon in the basement."

Ms. Keatley parked the car, and they all walked through the main entrance. Other quiz bowl teams were milling around the hallways, talking loudly. As soon as the Jewels entered, everyone grew quiet.

"I feel *awkward*," Lili whispered to Erin.

Erin pretended she didn't care as they walked toward the theater. "Hey, what's up?" she said with forced confidence to the other students. "Nice weather we're having, isn't it? Good day for a quiz bowl." The other kids stared, their mouths open, until the girls passed.

Jasmine turned bright red. "Erin!" she cried, but she was trying not to laugh.

One of the other team advisors waved to Ms. Keatley and motioned for her to come over. She turned to the girls.

"The competition starts in about fifteen minutes," she said. "I'll meet you inside. Just try to relax, okay?"

"We'll be totally chill," Erin promised.

Then another group of kids walked past, and they started whispering as soon as they saw the Jewels. That was too much for Jasmine.

"Come on," she said, grabbing Willow's arm. "Let's hang out somewhere else until this thing starts. I can't bear to go into that theater just yet!"

They turned a corner and found themselves in a quiet, empty hallway. Jasmine immediately relaxed.

"Everyone was looking at us! It's so awful!" she wailed.

"They'll be looking at us when we're onstage," Erin pointed out.

Jasmine groaned. "Don't remind me!"

The girls were quiet for a minute. They were all pretty nervous — even Erin, who tried to hide it. She distracted herself by looking at the photo display on the wall behind them: "A History of Atkinson Preparatory School."

"So this place was founded in 1816 by James Atkinson," she read aloud. "I guess he's Arthur Atkinson's great-great-great grandfather or something."

"Actually, he'd more likely be his great-great-great-great-*great* grandfather," Willow said. "If you do the math."

"Actually, I don't do the math," Erin said with a grin. "I leave that up to you."

Lili was looking at the photos, too. "Jazz, here's something to cheer you up. It's a pretty blue stone."

Curious, Jasmine walked to Lily's side. "It's a sapphire," she said, reading the card under the photo. "The Atkinson sapphire. The Atkinson family donated it to the school, but it was stolen in 1949. It says here that the sapphire is why Atkinson's school color is blue."

"Kind of like the Martha Washington ruby," Willow pointed out.

It seemed quiet all of a sudden, and they noticed that the sound of chatting in the other hallway had stopped.

"It must be starting," Willow said, and they hurried into the theater to find Ms. Keatley. At first, they watched the other teams compete while waiting for their turn. Jasmine saw Maddie, her friend from the Owls, sitting a few rows behind her. But when Jasmine turned to wave, Maddie acted like she didn't see her.

Jasmine sank into her seat, wishing it would suck her in and magically transport her home. No luck. The Jewels were called to the stage, and the whispering in the theater rose to a dull roar.

Lili reached into the messenger bag slung over her shoulder and pulled out what looked to be socks.

"I almost forgot!" she exclaimed. "I gave the team uniform another try. These are leg warmers. Each pair has our birthstones on them." She handed a set to Jasmine. "These have yellow topaz."

Erin was handed a pair fastened with turquoise, Willow received a set dotted with faux emeralds, and Lili's had fake pearls.

"Put them on!" Lili ordered. With the entire room watching, the girls slid on their leg warmers. One of Erin's got stuck in her shoe and she almost tumbled over.

Willow giggled. "Thanks, Lili."

"You're welcome!" she said. "Now let's go get 'em!"

They filed up the stage stairs, passing the Rivals. Isabel snorted derisively. "Nice leg warmers," she whispered, just loud enough for the Jewels to hear. Erin felt her cheeks turning bright red. Veronica caught her eye and gave her a small smile and a nod. Ryan and Aaron looked directly ahead and didn't make eye contact.

As the Jewels walked to their position, they spotted Ms. Keatley at the rear of the stage, having a heated discussion with Arthur Atkinson!

"I hope your team will play with honor and integrity today," he said pompously. "I could have petitioned to disqualify them."

Ms. Keatley was normally pretty calm, but in that moment, her eyes flashed. "On what grounds? They did nothing wrong. And I can assure you, my team always plays with honor and integrity!"

"Well, just know that I'll be watching them," he said before stalking off.

Willow felt Erin trembling with rage next to her.

"Relax." Willow tried to calm her friend, but she felt her own heart racing. "It's time to get started."

They quickly took their places behind four lecterns across the stage from the Rivals. Both teams faced the audience and the moderator stood at the edge of the stage, facing the teams. Willow cast a sideways glance at the Rivals, who looked supremely confident. Isabel met her stare, then rolled her eyes and looked away.

Furious, Willow focused her attention on the moderator as he introduced the teams. Then he started the match by reading the first question.

"Between which two planets does the orbit of Ceres occur?" he asked.

Astronomy! It was a subject Jasmine wasn't as familiar with, even though she had been brushing up on her sciences. Before she could search her memory, a buzzer sounded.

"Atkinson," the moderator said.

"Jupiter and Mars," Veronica answered.

"That is correct," the moderator replied.

The crowd in the theater clapped. Jasmine's shoulders slumped. Ryan flashed a triumphant look in the Jewels' direction. Then he and the Rivals quickly answered their bonus question. The points were already piling up.

"How did most people in France earn a living at the time of the French Revolution?" the moderator asked.

Easy, Erin thought. She had her hands gripped tightly together. She unclenched them and went to hit the buzzer, but her sweaty palm slid right off.

"The answer is farming or agriculture," Isabel replied confidently, shooting a "Take that!" look in Erin's direction. Erin's palms got even sweatier, and she wasn't alone. All the Jewels were quickly losing what little confidence they had going in, especially when the Rivals got the following bonus question right.

Then the moderator read the next toss-up question.

"Find the lowest common multiple of six, eight, and sixteen."

The girls turned to Willow. She always did awesome at math questions.

Willow began the calculations in her head. But then she caught Ryan Atkinson grinning at her. Was he laughing? She grew flustered and it took her longer to come up with the answer, giving Ryan the chance to buzz in first.

"The answer is forty-eight," he said self-assuredly.

"That is correct," the moderator affirmed.

All the girls were having trouble with the toss-up questions. Lili should have been able to ace the next one.

"Name the sixteenth-century Greek artist trained by monks who painted *The Burial of the Count of Orgaz*, among other masterpieces, in Spain."

But Lili wasn't paying attention. She was wondering if she'd really have to go to school at Atkinson. Besides the fashion-disaster uniforms, with her luck, she'd end up with a locker next to Isabel's. When Erin noticed her friend lost in thought, she gave her a nudge in the side. But it was too late. Aaron Santiago had buzzed in.

"El Greco," he answered.

"Correct." The moderator continued asking questions, but the Jewels couldn't get it together. With the exception of a couple of correct answers here and there, the Rivals decimated them.

After the match, the Rivals crossed the stage to shake hands with the Jewels.

"I'm sorry you didn't live up to your hype," Ryan said while shaking Willow's hand. "I was looking forward to the competition."

Willow felt some of her spirit returning.

"We're only down one match, Ryan," she said coolly. "We'll meet you guys again, and I don't think you'll be as lucky."

Ryan gave her a little salute before walking off.

Willow turned to her friends. "What is up with that guy?" she asked, angrily pounding her fist into her palm. "I'd like to see him get humiliated on the news and try to compete!"

"I don't think anything bothers him," Erin mused. "Maybe he's a robot. That would explain all those right answers."

Ms. Keatley walked up to them and ushered the girls backstage. "Come on. We can talk about this in private."

Jasmine collapsed into a folding chair. "That was a disaster!" she wailed, putting her head in her hands.

"The circumstances were unusual," Ms. Keatley said. "You girls will recover. I know it."

Willow was still angry. "I need to cool down," she told Ms. Keatley. "Can I go find some water?"

"I'll go with you," Lili said.

"There's a water fountain over by the dressing rooms," Ms. Keatley said, pointing. "Behind that red curtain."

Willow and Lili walked behind the curtain, which blocked the light filtering out from the stage, making it dark and hard to see. They heard voices and started to follow them, hoping they would lead to the dressing rooms. Suddenly, Willow recognized Isabel's French accent, and she sounded mad! Willow turned to Lili with a finger on her lips. Lili nodded. The two crept quietly toward the sound of Isabel's voice.

"It is not my fault!" Isabel said indignantly. "How was I to know?"

"You were supposed to check," Aaron said. "This plan was supposed to be foolproof."

"It is Jewel-proof," Isabel sneered. "Those girls couldn't find their way out of a paper bag."

"Forget about them," Ryan snapped. "We've got other things to worry about. I didn't want to hide it there in the first place. Now the exhibit is going on tour. We've got to get it back, and fast. I told you Minerva would have been a better choice. Even putting it on the neck of Columbia for all of DC to see would have been smarter."

Lili and Willow looked at each other, their eyes wide. Could the Rivals be talking about where they had hidden the ruby necklace?

Chapter Ten

$\mathcal{L}$ili stifled a cough. "We should go," they heard Ryan say. As soon as the Rivals went off in a different direction, Willow and Lili made their way back to the others. Ms. Keatley was talking to another advisor, so they pulled Erin and Jasmine aside.

"You won't believe what we just heard!" Lili whispered excitedly. She quickly filled them in.

"They didn't mention the ruby, did they?" Jasmine asked.

"No, but what else could they be talking about?" Willow wondered.

"I'm not saying anything to anyone about it," Jasmine said fiercely. "Not after what happened last time."

"Besides, the police searched the whole school and the Rivals' houses and proved they didn't take the ruby, didn't they?" Erin asked.

Willow shook her head. "That only means that they didn't hide the ruby at home or at school. Think about it. They made a big deal about how they didn't have the ruby. Maybe that was their plan. They hid the ruby someplace no one would imagine, and in the meantime everyone thinks they're innocent and we're losers."

Jasmine looked skeptical. "You mean Arthur Atkinson was in on it?"

"Why not?" Lili chimed in. "I mean, a bunch of sixth graders couldn't steal a valuable jewel all by themselves, could they?"

"Exactly," Jasmine said. "Which is why we shouldn't be trying to act like detectives, either."

"But we have to!" Willow pleaded. "You're right. We can't go to Principal Frederickson with this, because no one would believe us. But we can at least check it out. And if we're right, everyone will know we're not losers."

Jasmine sighed. "I guess, as long as we don't say anything until we're sure. . . ."

Erin was strangely quiet the whole time. "Could it be possible?" she said, mostly to herself. "It seems so unbelievable."

"What?" Lili asked.

"You said that Ryan mentioned Minerva. The fresco at the Capitol Building shows six scenes, each depicting Roman gods and god-desses," Erin explained. "One of those goddesses is Minerva, the Roman goddess of crafts and wisdom."

"Oh, yes! The painting on the ceiling!" Lili said in agreement. "But how would you hide a ruby there?"

"That's not all," Erin said. "He also mentioned the neck of Columbia, right? *Columbia* is the name of the statue on top of the Capitol. Not one, but two references to the Capitol Building. It seems like more than a coincidence."

"It's worth checking out," Willow said.

In the car ride back to school, Ms. Keatley tried to cheer the girls up.

"You know what would help?" Erin asked. "Another field trip!"

"Could we go to the Capitol Building tomorrow?" Willow asked. "For more research?"

Ms. Keatley sighed. "I still haven't gotten to see the John Adams miniseries yet."

"Please, please, Ms. Keatley," Lili begged.

"Oh, all right," Ms. Keatley replied. "I'll ask your parents when they pick you up. You've all had such an awful day, I'd do anything to put a smile on your faces."

The next morning, the girls met again at the Metrorail train station. But this time, the vibe in the air felt more serious than fun.

Jasmine yawned. She had had bad dreams again the previous night. In this nightmare, Principal Frederickson wore a beret and legwarmers as she chased Jasmine around, demanding the ruby back in a French accent.

Ms. Keatley looked tired, too. "I stayed up half the night watching *John Adams*. I couldn't turn it off." She clutched a big cup of coffee in her hand.

The train pulled into the station and everyone got on. Before they knew it, they were once again back at the National Mall. They walked to the east end, toward the impressive, towering white Capitol Building. The central dome rose above a rotunda and was flanked by the two wings of the building.

Willow pointed to the top of the dome. "There's *Columbia*."

Erin pulled a pair of minibinoculars out of her bag and trained them on the statue. Lili laughed.

"Erin, do you have a bag full of detective tools in there?" she asked.

"That's the best part of being a detective," Erin replied. "All the cool stuff they use. I'm saving up for night-vision goggles."

Willow took the binoculars from Erin. "Did you see anything?"

"I don't think so. Hey, did you know the statue is also referred to as the statue of freedom?" Erin asked.

"Now I do," Willow said. "Either way, she's pretty cool-looking."

She gazed up at the bronze statue of a young woman wearing a feather-fringed helmet. In her right hand, she held the hilt of a sheathed sword. In her left, a laurel wreath and a shield. But no ruby.

Willow lowered the binoculars and frowned. "We might as well go inside and check out the Minerva clue."

They got in the long security line at the visitors' center, but it moved quickly. While they waited, Ms. Keatley read from a guidebook. "'The US Capitol is a massive building, with five hundred forty rooms divided among five levels. The site is home to the Senate, House of Representatives, Supreme Court, Library of Congress, and the US Botanic Garden.' Oh dear, where do we start?"

"Let's take a tour," Jasmine suggested.

The tour began with a short film about the history of the Capitol and Congress. The tour guide, an older woman with a gold emblem on her blazer, took them to the National Statuary Hall next.

"This was the meeting place for the US House of Representatives for nearly fifty years," she explained. "Now it is the main exhibition space for the national statuary collection."

The girls gazed around in amazement at the large, two-story semicircular room. From the gold ceiling hung an elaborate chandelier. And there were marble and bronze statues of famous Americans, donated by each of the fifty states, all around the room. As the guide talked, the girls carefully looked at each statue. Lili even stuck her head into an unused fireplace.

"Nothing here," she concluded.

The tour continued. The Jewels kept on the lookout as they browsed galleries displaying artifacts from the Library of Congress and the National Archives. But when they reached the Rotunda, they were all extra alert.

"The Rotunda is the symbolic as well as the physical heart of the United States Capitol," the guide said. "It connects the House and Senate sides of the building and is visited by thousands of people each day. It is located below the dome and is the tallest part of the Capitol."

Erin's jaw dropped. She almost forgot about the ruby as she stood under the swirling, massive ceiling. High above, at the very top of the dome, was the large fresco painting *The Apotheosis of Washington*, which showed George Washington hanging out in the clouds with some Roman gods and famous people from history. It contained the scene with Minerva. Erin groaned out loud. "There's no way the Rivals could have gotten up there," she whispered to Willow.

"Yeah," Willow agreed. "But let me take a closer look."

She pulled out Erin's binoculars and looked up. After a few minutes, she lowered them and shook her head. "Nothing."

The girls finished the tour, dejected. Ms. Keatley was puzzled. "I thought this would cheer you up!"

On the way back to the train, the girls hung back, letting Ms. Keatley walk ahead so they could talk.

"It's hopeless!" Erin moaned. "We should give up."

"I hate to say it, but I agree with Erin," Lili said sadly. "This was a waste of time."

Jasmine met Willow's eyes and nodded. "We should just concentrate on the next quiz bowl and put this behind us."

Willow sighed. "I guess we'll never get the ruby back!"

Chapter Eleven

The next day, Aaron Santiago walked up to the table Eli and Zane were sitting at in the Atkinson Prep cafeteria.

"Did you guys hear?" he asked. "They're filming *Curse of the Black Tiger Two*! I can't wait to see it!"

Eli was suspicious. After all, he knew Aaron and Ryan had been lying about seeing the first movie.

"Cool," Zane replied. "I wonder if I can get a part?" He held up his hands in a classic kung fu stance.

Aaron laughed. "Yeah, that'd be great. Well, gotta go. Just thought you guys would want to know."

As he turned to leave, a piece of paper fluttered from his pocket to the floor.

"Hey! You dropped something," Eli said loudly. But Aaron didn't seem to hear him and kept walking.

Zane scooped it up. "It's just an old ticket stub," he said. "I'll throw it out."

"Wait! Let me see that," Eli reached out his hand. He read the paper. "Very interesting."

After school, Eli popped his head into Lili's room. All of the Jewels were there, studying for the next quiz bowl. They wanted to redeem themselves after their last disastrous match against the Rivals.

"Go away, Eli! We're busy," Lili said.

"Okay, if you don't want to hear about how weird Aaron Santiago was acting today, fine." He made like he was going to walk away.

"Wait!" Willow called. "What happened?"

Eli filled them in. "When he was leaving, he dropped a ticket stub to the National Zoo. But this is where it gets stranger. The ticket stub was dated the same day the ruby was stolen from Martha Washington." He held up the stub.

Erin grabbed it from his hands and studied it. "It is!"

"If Aaron was really at the zoo that day, why would he lie about going to the movies?" Jasmine wondered.

"Maybe the Rivals hid the ruby at the zoo!" Lili cried.

Erin laughed. "And Mei Xiang the panda is wearing it?"

Willow scowled. "That's weird," she said. "I just got a Chatter update that Veronica uploaded a new pic." She peered at her phone. "And it looks like it was taken at the zoo!"

She held up her phone to show a photo of two large brown turtles.

"Let me see." Jasmine held out her hand. She studied the photo. "Those are Aldabra giant tortoises."

"I'm on it!" Lili jumped on her computer and began typing furiously. "Here they are!" She pointed to the screen, which showed the National Zoo's website. "There is an Aldabra tortoise exhibit there."

Jasmine groaned. "I thought we weren't going to get involved anymore. I've had enough humiliation to last a lifetime, thanks very much."

"What would it hurt to take a trip to the zoo?" Erin asked. "Besides, you love the zoo!"

"Tomorrow is a half day at school because of teacher conferences," Willow said thoughtfully. "Maybe my mom can take us, if we help out with my little brothers."

On Tuesday afternoon, the girls piled into Mrs. Albern's minivan along with Willow's three younger brothers: two-year-old Jason, six-year-old Michael, and eight-year-old Alex. With their dark brown hair and big brown eyes, all three boys resembled their big sister.

"It was so nice of you all to suggest this outing." Mrs. Albern smiled. "The boys love the zoo! Although it looks like it might rain."

She glanced up at the sky with concern. "Does everyone have an umbrella?"

With Mrs. Albern pushing Jaden in a stroller, they walked through the visitors' center and started their trip on the Asia Trail. They *ooh*ed and *aah*ed over the adorable otters and red panda cubs and had a contest to see who could spot the clouded leopard first. Next up was the famous giant panda exhibit, with Tian Tian and Mei Xiang.

"What goes black, white, black, white, black, white?" Michael asked.

"What?" Lili asked.

"A panda rolling down a hill!" Michael cracked himself up, and Alex joined in.

Although Jasmine loved the zoo, she felt herself growing impatient. Willow noticed her friend was anxious. "We'll be there soon," she promised.

They made their way through the elephant exhibit and past the monkeys and great apes cages before arriving at the Reptile House. In the area just before the reptiles, there was the tortoise exhibit with a low fence running around it.

"Easy to get into," Erin said. "Not like the dome of the Capitol Building!"

They scanned the exhibit. Two giant tortoises sat inside, just like in Veronica's picture. But this time, something was different.

On both of the turtles' shells was written in chalk: "Ha."

" 'Ha, Ha,' " Michael read aloud. "Is that their names, Mom? Ha?"

Just then, the skies opened up and it began raining. The downpour washed the chalk off the shells.

Jasmine turned to the rest of the Jewels, her wet hair plastered on her face. "Ha-ha," she said bitterly. "It looks like the joke's on us!"

Chapter Twelve

When they got back to Hallytown, the girls gathered around Willow's kitchen table, drinking hot cocoa that Mrs. Albern had made for them.

"So do you really think the Rivals wrote 'Ha Ha' on those tortoise shells?" Lili asked, shaking her head.

"Who else would do that?" Erin pointed out. "They're mocking us!"

"It *does* seem like a setup," Willow said thoughtfully. "First Aaron drops the ticket right in front of Eli. Then Veronica posts the photo of the turtles. It's like they were leading us there."

Jasmine looked miserable. "Well, I don't think it was funny."

"But don't you see?" Erin said, her face brightening. "This proves they're the thieves! They just gave themselves away!"

Willow shook her head. "All it proves is that they're trying to embarrass us even more."

"Willow's right," Jasmine said. "They know we suspect them, so they've turned this into a game."

"But they *didn't* know you guys were listening the day of the quiz bowl, when they were talking about their foolproof plan, or whatever," Erin pointed out. "I am so sure they're the ones who stole the necklace!"

"Maybe, but we can't prove it," Willow reminded her.

The girls stared into their mugs of cocoa, dejected. Willow's mom walked in and noticed their sad expressions.

"You girls have been so gloomy all day," she remarked. "I know this whole situation with Atkinson must be difficult for you. I think you need to clear your minds and get a fresh start. Hey, there's a free beginners' yoga class at the community center tonight. Why don't you all stay for supper and I'll take you there? As long as it's okay with your parents."

"Yoga?" Erin asked skeptically. "Don't you have to twist up your body like a pretzel or something?"

Mrs. Albern laughed. "Only when you get really good. Seriously, though, this class is very gentle and relaxing. I think it would be good for you. And I've got a huge batch of veggie chili working in the slow cooker."

"Mmm, I love your chili!" Erin said happily. "I'll twist my arms in knots if we get to eat that."

"Sounds good," Lili agreed.

Jasmine sighed. "It's worth a try. I would love to erase the last week from my brain if I could!"

After eating dinner with the Alberns and changing into some sweats borrowed from Willow, the girls found themselves in a small room with smooth wood floors at the community center. Soft music played in the background as the yoga instructor, a young woman named Seline, talked to her students in a soothing voice.

"This next position is called downward dog," Seline said. "We're starting from the tabletop position. Tuck your toes under, and press your hands into the floor."

Like the other girls, Lili was on her yoga mat with her knees on the floor, her hands flat on the mat, her elbows straight, and her back as flat as the top of a table. She could hear Erin giggling next to her. Normally, she would be giggling right along, but she had to admit that she was kind of enjoying the yoga thing. It really was making her feel calm.

"Now straighten your legs to come up into the pose," Seline directed, rising from the mat and forming an arched shape with her body.

Lili did the same, and now her head was upside down. Through the space between her feet she could see the plain white wall behind her.

"Let's hold this pose for five breaths," Seline said. Her voice was loud yet soothing at the same time. "Breathe in. Breathe out. Breathe in. Breathe out. . . ."

Lili felt more and more relaxed. Thoughts from the last few days kept drifting into her brain, and she tried to let them pass on through without dwelling on them, like Seline had instructed at the start of class.

Turtles . . . the Capitol . . . joke's on you . . . Minerva . . .

Minerva. That name stuck for some reason. And then it hit her.

"I've got it!" she cried, not realizing she was saying the words out loud. Most of the students were too polite to laugh, but Erin was cracking up next to her.

"Very good, Lili," Seline said. "Now let's smoothly release the pose so that we're back down on hands and knees."

For the remainder of the class, Lili could barely concentrate. She was sure she had figured out something important, and she couldn't wait to tell her friends. When Seline finally dismissed them, Lili ran up to the Jewels.

"Wow, Lili, you really got into it," Erin teased.

"No, I didn't," Lili said. "I mean, I did, but that's not why I shouted like that. I think I figured something out."

"What do you mean?" Jasmine asked.

"Well, Ryan mentioned Minerva, right?" Lili asked, and Willow nodded.

"Well, I thought of *another* Minerva. One that has to do with jewels," Lili told them. "It's my favorite thing in the National Museum of American History. It's called the 'Minerva' Dress, and it was designed by Oscar de la Renta. It's all gold and shimmery and everything. Maybe he was talking about that!"

"Hey, you could be right!" Erin agreed.

"Yes, but Ryan said that they *didn't* hide it in Minerva," Willow reminded them.

"Right, but maybe they hid it in another dress, and that's why they mentioned it," Jasmine suggested.

"Well, there are lots of dresses in the museum," Lili pointed out.

"It's too bad there isn't a Martha Washington dress. Now, *that* would be obvious!" Jasmine joked.

"But there is!" Lili said, her voice rising with excitement. "There's a First Ladies exhibit at the history museum. I've seen it a few times. There is definitely a Martha Washington dress there."

Willow took out her phone and started typing. "You're right," she said after a minute. "There's a Martha Washington dress. And here's something interesting. The exhibit is closing down next Friday because they're going to be sending it on tour!"

"That's got to be what the Rivals were talking about," Jasmine realized. "Ryan said the exhibit was going on tour! He must have meant *this* exhibit."

"So they've got to get the ruby necklace back before next Friday," Lili said, putting the pieces together.

Erin's blue eyes were on fire. "No, *we've* got to get the ruby back," she said. "It's the only way to clear our names."

The girls were quiet for a moment as they thought about what this meant.

"It could be another trick," Jasmine warned.

"Maybe," Willow agreed. "But it couldn't hurt to check it out."

Erin grinned. "I think it's time for another field trip!"

Chapter Thirteen

"Honestly, girls, these field trips are getting to be a bit much," Ms. Keatley complained as they climbed up the steps to the third floor of the National Museum of American History.

Willow and the other girls were already a few steps ahead, eager to get to the First Ladies exhibit. Willow turned back to answer her. "I just read an article that says that immersion learning is fifteen percent more effective than other methods when you're studying for quiz bowl," she said. It wasn't exactly true, but she knew Ms. Keatley would like the idea.

"Immersion learning?" Lili asked, and Erin nudged her.

"It's learning from experiences, instead of just reading books," Willow explained. "Like going to museums."

"I understand the benefits," Ms. Keatley said as they reached the top of the stairs. "But it does take up a lot of — oh look, Eleanor Roosevelt's gown!"

She drifted away to examine the dress, leaving the girls to themselves.

"I know where the Martha dress is," Lili said, leading them to it.

The First Ladies exhibit was arranged along the wall of the museum, with a separate display area for each of the first ladies that were included. At the start of each display were glass-protected shelves that held personal items owned by each president's wife, topped with a portrait. To the right of that was a dress owned by each woman, along with a plaque that told about the dress.

"Here's Martha," Willow said, pointing up to the portrait, which showed Martha in her younger days, with a graceful long neck and her short hair held back by a jeweled headband. "And here's the dress."

The pale peach dress had a long, full skirt with a white lace collar and cuffs.

"Isn't it beautiful? The fabric seems painted," Lili said. "Those look like butterflies and flowers. So pretty!"

"It says the dress is painted silk," Jasmine said, reading the plaque.

"Um, hello," Erin hissed. "Necklace, remember?"

A glittering ruby necklace sat on top of a tall, thin pedestal right next to the dress.

"Oh my gosh, that's it!" Lili cried, and Willow shushed her.

"Maybe, or maybe it's a reproduction, like the plaque says," Willow pointed out. "Jasmine, do you recognize it?"

Jasmine frowned. "Well, it *looks* like the necklace," she said. "The color is deep, and the luster, or shine, is good. But I can't really be sure."

"So if this is the real necklace, then the Rivals switched it with the reproduction?" Lili asked.

Willow nodded. "It's perfect. Nobody would ever think this was the real one."

"It's too bad I can't compare this to the reproduction," Jasmine remarked. "I might have been able to notice some differences."

Erin's eyes lit up. "But you can!" she cried. "Be right back!"

The girls exchanged puzzled glances as their friend hurried out of the exhibit. They stood there for a moment, not sure what to do, when a security guard in a blue uniform walked past them. He was a small man with a bushy gray mustache and a cap pulled over his eyes. He nodded to the girls as he passed.

"Let's move around a little," Jasmine whispered to Lili and Willow. "So we don't look suspicious."

They nervously wandered around the exhibit until Erin came back a few minutes later, breathless. She handed Jasmine a program for the First Ladies exhibit.

"Look on page thirty-five," she said.

Jasmine leafed through the program and smiled. "I get it. There's a great photo of the reproduction necklace right here."

Erin nodded. "I hope it helps. I spent my whole allowance on it."

The girls casually walked back to the exhibit, and Jasmine studied the necklace, comparing it with the photo in the book. After a few minutes she broke out into a huge grin.

"Got it!" she whispered. "See the setting around the main ruby? In the reproduction, it has six prongs, right? Now count the prongs on the necklace that's here."

The girls silently counted.

"Five!" Erin said.

Jasmine nodded. "The real necklace was missing one of the prongs, but it was kept in its original condition. In the reproduction, they used all six prongs. The necklace we're looking at now is the real one!"

The girls were quiet for a moment as they realized what a big deal this was.

"So what do we do now?" Erin asked finally. "Reach in and grab it?"

"No way," Lili said, looking around nervously. "Someone would see us."

Willow looked thoughtful. "So how did the Rivals make the switch?"

Erin shrugged "Who knows? But I just thought of one good thing. At least they haven't stolen it back yet!"

Willow turned to Jasmine. "What do you think? Is this enough proof?"

"Maybe," Jasmine said hesitantly. "Just maybe."

"Then let's tell Principal Frederickson tomorrow," Willow suggested. "Let's see what she wants to do."

Chapter Fourteen

"Absolutely not, girls," Principal Frederickson said before school began the next morning. "I will not pursue this matter any further. The idea that our necklace is in a national museum display is completely preposterous!"

"But we have proof!" Willow protested. "The prongs!"

Principal Frederickson sighed. "To my knowledge, the necklace setting was never missing a prong."

"But I *know* it was," Jasmine interjected. "I sketched it so many times!"

Principal Frederickson slid a white envelope across her desk. "Arthur Atkinson has requested that you four make a formal apology for making false accusations. I am very saddened by the theft. But I strongly suggest that you girls stop accusing the Atkinson students. I know Arthur Atkinson well, and he'll sue you for slander."

"That's not fair! He can't sue us if what we say is true," Erin protested. "And the exhibit is closing soon, and the Rivals know it.

They're going to get the ruby back, and then we'll *never* be able to prove it."

The first bell of the morning rang, and Principal Frederickson stood up.

"Please go to class, girls," she said sternly. "This matter is over. And, I have to say, I'm disappointed in you four."

The girls left the office and walked outside the main building.

"So, I guess that's that," Willow said with a sigh.

"This is *not* over," Jasmine said, surprising everyone. "A formal apology? How dare they! We have got to clear our names."

"But how?" Lili asked. "That's what we've been trying to do all this time!"

Jasmine lowered her voice. "I don't know. But we've got to do something."

Erin grinned. "Let's do what the Rivals did. Let's just take it."

"And then what?" Willow asked. "We'll get arrested for jewelry theft!"

"No, we won't," Erin pointed out. "Because they can easily test to see if the rubies are real. And we're only taking what's rightfully ours as Martha Washington students."

Willow shook her head. "I don't know."

"Let's meet at my house tonight," Lili suggested. "Maybe Eli can help us."

* * *

"All those displays are protected by alarms," Eli said, typing on his laptop. "It's like an invisible fence. Once you cross the front of the display, an alarm goes off."

Eli sat on a pile of clothes on the edge of Lili's bed while his sister and the rest of the Jewels sat on the fluffy purple rug on the floor. Lili's messy bedroom was a lot like her personality: colorful and fun. Almost every inch of wall space was covered with posters, Lili's sketches, stickers, and pictures of clothes cut out from magazines.

"So, we could grab it and run really fast," Erin suggested.

Eli shook his head. "There are guards everywhere. And when the alarms go off, I think the exits automatically lock or something. At least, I saw that in a movie."

Erin frowned and went back to the book in her lap.

"Anything in there that can help us?" Willow asked.

Erin patted the stack of old books she had taken out from the school library. "Not really. I guess I thought if I knew more about Martha Washington we could find a way into the exhibit. But I should have taken out books about jewel thieves instead!"

"*We're* not the thieves," Jasmine corrected her. "The Rivals are. We're just taking back what they stole."

"Only if we have a plan," Erin reminded her. "Lili, maybe you need to turn upside down again. That worked last time."

"Why not?" Lili replied. She climbed up on her bed, lay down on her back, and hung her head over the edge of the bed.

"Anything?" Erin asked after a minute.

"Not yet," Lili admitted. "Mostly I've got a headache. But I — help! I'm slipping!"

Even though Eli was right next to her, he was typing on his laptop and couldn't grab his sister's legs. The girls rushed over to catch Lili before she fell, but bumped into her instead. They ended up giggling in a heap on the floor.

"What is all that commotion up there?" Lili's grandmother yelled from downstairs.

"Sorry," Lili apologized, sitting up. "Guess that didn't work."

"Maybe it *did* work," Erin said. "A commotion could be just what we need!"

"What do you mean?" Jasmine asked.

"I think I get it," Willow said. "If the alarm goes off on another display, then nobody will notice if we reach into the Martha Washington one."

Erin nodded. "Exactly. So if we cause a commotion at one display, Willow can reach in and grab the necklace."

Willow's eyes got big. "Me? Why me?"

"Because you're the fastest," Erin pointed out.

Eli nodded. "True."

"Don't worry," Erin said. "I'll stand in front of the display to block what you're doing."

Willow sighed. "I guess. So what kind of commotion can we cause?"

Lili waved her hand wildly. "Oh, I could do that part! Like, I could be sketching one of the other dresses all the way at the end of the exhibit, and then I'll, like, lean in close to get a good look, and then . . . *bam*! I'll fall right over."

"And one of us could try to help her up, and then trip over her or something," Jasmine suggested.

"And maybe some screaming," Erin added. "Screaming is always good."

Eli closed his laptop. "You know, that just might work."

"And then we can take the necklace to the police, and they'll test it and prove it's the real one," Willow said.

"What if they think we're the ones who took it?" Jasmine asked nervously.

"We'll show them all our proof," Willow said. "They'll have to believe us."

The room was silent again.

"So we're really doing this," Jasmine said, as though she was trying to convince herself.

"Well, we can do this, or we can make a formal apology to the Rivals," Erin said.

Jasmine's hazel eyes narrowed. "I'll ask my mom to drive us."

Chapter Fifteen

The next day seemed to drag on forever. The Jewels sat in class, worrying if their plan would work or not. Jasmine's foot tapped nervously all day, until her math teacher begged her to stop. Erin dropped her food tray at lunch, dousing Willow with ketchup. Lili found herself daydreaming so much she didn't notice when her teachers called on her. And Willow, usually the star of gym class, drifted aimlessly around the basketball court, unable to follow the game. When the last bell of the day rang, the girls packed up and made it outside in record speed to meet Jasmine's mom.

Willow exhaled as they walked to the parking lot. "Finally. I thought we'd never get out of there!"

"Me, too!" Lili said as her phone beeped. She took it out of her bag and read a text message. "Eli says the Rivals are on the move. He overheard them talking and thinks they are going to the history museum today, too!"

"We've got to hurry!" Erin cried. They raced toward the car and piled in furiously.

"Whoa! Where's the fire?" Mrs. Johnson asked, surprised.

Jasmine caught her breath. "We're just really excited to get to the museum, Mom!"

It seemed like an eternity, but they made it to the National Museum of American History quickly.

"Are you sure no one wants to come to the Music and the American Experience exhibit with me?" Mrs. Johnson asked.

"No thanks, Mom," Jasmine said hurriedly. "We'll meet you in an hour at the café, like we planned." The girls started running toward the steps leading to the third floor.

"No running in the museum, please," a security guard told them. He was the same short man with the bushy mustache they had seen the other day.

"Oops, sorry," Lili said as the girls slowed their pace to a fast walk.

"We need to keep our eyes out for the Rivals," Willow said in a low voice as they walked up the stairs. "If they are here, then we know they're trying to steal the ruby back!"

"And it's up to us to stop them!" Jasmine said.

The girls reached the First Ladies exhibit quickly. Erin began rushing toward the ruby, when Willow put her hand up to stop her.

"We've got to act like everything's normal," she whispered to her friends. "Let's get into position. Remember, it's up to Lili and Jasmine to cause a distraction nearby. Then while Erin covers me, I'll grab the ruby. But we've got to keep our cool."

Willow and Erin pretended to stroll leisurely toward the Martha Washington section, but their eyes were carefully searching the crowd. It was a busy day. A lot of tour groups were visiting, and the exhibit was crowded with noisy kids and their harried teachers. But there was no sign of any of the Rivals. They reached the Martha Washington display and stared at the ruby. Erin counted the prongs and gave a thumbs-up to Willow. The real ruby was still there!

Meanwhile, Lili and Jasmine made their way to the display of Sarah Polk, wife of the eleventh president of the United States, James Polk. It was a few displays down from the Martha Washington dress and ruby. Lili sat on a bench in front of the dress and pulled out her sketch pad. Jasmine pretended to be entranced by the dress as well, but she was really searching the crowd.

Lili took out a pencil and began to sketch the light blue brocaded silk dress. It was woven with a design of poinsettias, and the front of the gown had elaborate pleating and large bows. Lili's brow puckered as she concentrated on getting the shape onto paper when her phone once again let out a beep.

She quickly read the message and looked up at Jasmine, alarmed.

"Eli said he forgot about the cameras!" she whispered frantically. "There are several here, aimed at the displays."

Jasmine looked up. A video camera sat in the corner of the ceiling, its red light blinking as it slowly turned around the room.

"It's moving slowly," Jasmine said. "If we time it just right, we should be okay. I'll go let Willow know."

Jasmine moved through the crowd as Lili resumed her sketching. Suddenly, Lili felt a tap on her shoulder. She almost hit the ceiling when she turned and saw her grandmother!

"Obaasan!" Lili cried, shocked.

"Why, Lili, you almost jumped off of that bench," her grandmother, Mrs. Takahashi, replied with a clicking of her tongue. "I bet you've been drinking soda. All of that caffeine and sugar is no good for you. I keep telling you that."

"No, Obaasan, I haven't . . ." Lili almost began to argue but changed her mind. "What are you doing here?"

"The community center organized a trip for the seniors. And I'm so glad I bumped into you. I saw the most beautiful necklace in the gift shop and was thinking of getting it for your mother, but I am not sure if she has something similar," Mrs. Takahashi explained. "Come with me. You've got a great eye for these types of things. I know you'll remember."

"The gift shop is on the first floor! I'm waiting for my friends," Lili said, the panic creeping into her voice. How was she going to get out of this? Her eyes swept the room, and she spotted Jasmine talking to Willow.

Jasmine had quickly explained Eli's text. Willow looked at the cameras and thought it over.

"I agree with you," she said to Jasmine. "If we time it just right, we should be fine. Start the distraction right after the camera sweeps by."

Jasmine nodded and made her way back to the Polk dress, just in time to see Lili being dragged away by her grandmother!

"Friends, friends, you're always with your friends!" Mrs. Takahashi was saying. "It will only take a second."

Lili locked eyes with Jasmine helplessly. Jasmine stood stunned as her friend left the room, taking all their hopes with her.

Chapter Sixteen

"Did you see that?" Jasmine asked Erin and Willow. "Lili's grandmother just took her away."

"Oh no! Do you think she knows what we're doing?" Erin asked nervously.

"If she did, she would probably have come for all of us, right?" Willow asked, but she didn't sound sure.

Jasmine started to frantically pace back and forth. "There's no way we can do this now. We should get out of here!"

"We don't have to," Erin said. "I'll take Lili's place. I can make a really good commotion."

"Then who will watch Willow's back?" Jasmine asked.

"She doesn't need anyone. She's fast," Erin replied.

Both girls looked at Willow, who glanced at the necklace inside the display, calculating.

"Should be easy," Willow said. "Let's stick to the plan."

Erin and Lili headed back to the Sarah Polk display. Lili had left her sketchbook on the bench, so Erin sat down and picked it up. Then she looked at Jasmine, alarmed.

"What is it?" Jasmine hissed.

"I forgot something," Erin said. "I can't draw."

"Then just pretend or something," Jasmine urged. "Or maybe it's a sign. Maybe we should just forget about the whole thing."

"No, no, I got this!" Erin said confidently. She picked up the pencil and began to move it around the paper. "Just give me a signal when the camera's pointing away from Martha Washington."

"What kind of signal?" Jasmine asked.

Erin looked thoughtful. "Um, how about a peace sign?" she asked, holding up two fingers.

Jasmine nodded. "Okay. Peace sign."

Jasmine nervously paced back and forth, eyeing the video camera. The first time it swung away from the Martha dress, Jasmine almost made the peace sign, but then she noticed that the security guard was all the way down the hall, near Willow.

I'll just wait until he comes closer this way, she reasoned. Her palms were starting to sweat, and she rubbed her hands on her leggings. When they had first hatched this plan, she thought she had the easiest job. But now it seemed like the most important. If she didn't time things just right, they could be in big trouble.

Erin shot a questioning glance at her, but Jasmine just shook her head and kept pacing. The security guard was moving now, slowly making his way down the room. She looked up to see where the camera was, and . . . saw a woman with upswept hair wearing an elegant suit walking up the staircase to the third floor.

Principal Frederickson? But it couldn't be! They couldn't go through with the plan! Not now! Panicked, Jasmine spun around to run and tell Erin, and tripped over the lace of her left boot.

The fall seemed to happen in slow motion. She got that sick feeling in her stomach at the moment when she realized she couldn't steady herself and was *definitely* going down. Her arms flailed wildly to find something to hold on to, but there was nothing. She fell facedown into the Sarah Polk dress!

Whoo-ee! Whoo-ee! Whoo-ee! The shrill alarm pierced the air. Erin tossed the pencil and sketchbook to the floor and raced up to the display.

"Help! Help! Help!" she yelled as loud as she could. "I think she's hurt!"

Everyone at the exhibit turned to look at the Sarah Polk display, and that's when Willow made her move. When she was sure no one was looking, she quickly vaulted over the knee-high barrier in front of the Martha Washington display and grabbed the necklace off the pedestal. Then she leaped back out. Willow stood there for a second, not really believing that she held the ruby in her hand. She had done it!

Then she felt a tap on her shoulder.

"Hand it over," a muffled voice said.

Willow spun around to see the security guard with the bushy mustache in front of her. Her heart nearly jumped from her chest. She was caught!

With a trembling hand, she placed the ruby into the man's outstretched palm. A strange thought entered her mind.

For an old man, his hands are very small and smooth.

She looked back up at the guard's face and he tipped his hat back, revealing an equally smooth forehead and two young brown eyes. He winked, and at that moment Willow recognized him.

"Aaron Santiago!" she cried, stunned.

The Rivals member quickly tucked the ruby necklace into his pocket, put another ruby necklace on the platform, and then hurried away.

It took a few seconds for Willow to process what had happened.

She had taken the necklace. Aaron had taken it from her. And now he was getting away.

She raced down the exhibit, where she found two real security guards helping Jasmine get to her feet.

"Are you sure you're okay, young lady?" one of the men asked her. "We could take you to our first aid center."

"No, no, I'm fine," Jasmine insisted. "My mom's here. I'll just go find her."

Erin caught Willow's eye, and Willow motioned for them to hurry up. Erin grabbed Jasmine's arm.

"Yes, actually, her mom is probably looking for us," Erin said, pulling Jasmine away. "Thanks, officers."

The security guards shrugged at each other and the girls walked off.

"So, did you get it?" Erin hissed to Willow.

"I did," Willow replied. "But then Aaron Santiago got it. We have to go after him!"

Willow took off running, and Jasmine and Erin exchanged puzzled glances before following her.

"That's him, in the security guard uniform," Willow said, pointing to Aaron as he ran down the stairs. "He's probably headed for the exit that goes right out to the National Mall."

They bolted down the stairs after him, but Aaron had gotten a good head start. At the bottom of the stairs, they saw him bump into a girl with short blond hair before turning left toward the America on the Move exhibit.

"That's Isabel!" Jasmine realized. "Aaron must have given her the necklace!"

By the time they reached the bottom of the stairs, Isabel was hurrying down the next staircase to the first floor. They saw Ryan waiting at the bottom for her, and she bumped into him before making a sharp right turn, the same way Aaron had.

By now the girls had almost caught up. Ryan made his way across the crowded first floor, and Willow reached out to grab him just as he made it to the exit.

"Girls! What are you doing?"

Willow froze. Jasmine's mom walked up to them with Lili at her side.

"I found Lili in the museum store with her grandmother, and we were just going upstairs to find you, but then I saw you heading outside. You know better than to leave the museum without me," she said, with a stern look at Jasmine.

"We just needed some . . . air," Erin explained. "We weren't going anywhere."

Mrs. Johnson shook her head. "Honestly, I expected more from you girls. You're in sixth grade now."

Next to Mrs. Johnson, Lili gave Erin a curious look: *Did you get it?* Erin shook her head slowly. Jasmine looked like she might cry, and Willow's fists were curled tightly as she gazed out the exit onto Constitution Avenue. Ryan was nowhere in sight.

The Rivals had won — again.

Chapter Seventeen

On the car ride back to Hallytown, the girls frantically texted one another.

What happened? typed Lili.

We all need to talk. Library after dinner? Willow replied. The girls often met at the Hallytown Library to do homework together.

In the driver's seat, Mrs. Johnson shook her head. "Are you girls really texting one another when you could just be talking? Honestly, I don't understand this generation sometimes."

"We're just taking notes from the museum, Mom," Jasmine said quickly. "Hey, is it okay if I go to the library tonight to do homework? We're all meeting there."

"Of course. It's nice to see how you girls support one another," her mother answered.

Willow, Lili, and Erin texted their parents and got permission. A few hours later, they met at a small table in the Hallytown Library, the one hidden behind the reference section. Lili had brought Eli with her. After all his help, he was definitely an honorary Jewel team member now.

"So, first of all, Lili, what happened with you and your grandmother?" Willow whispered as the friends huddled around the table.

"She dragged me to the gift shop with her," Lili said. "So, did you guys dump the plan?"

Erin shook her head. "No, I took your place. I was waiting for a signal from Jasmine, but she tripped into the Sarah Polk display instead."

"It was an accident!" Jasmine insisted. "I saw Principal Frederickson on the stairs, I swear."

Willow shook her head. "Wait. Are you sure? Maybe you just thought it was her."

Jasmine sighed. "I . . . I think so. But I guess it doesn't matter now. I messed up."

"You totally did not!" Erin told her. "You made a great commotion. It worked just like we planned. Willow was able to get the necklace."

"And then a security guard asked me to hand it over," Willow said. "But it wasn't really a security guard. It was Aaron Santiago from the Rivals! He put the reproduction back in the display and ran off, and as you guys know, I couldn't catch him."

Erin almost jumped out of her seat at the news. "Aaron disguised as a security guard?" she asked, surprised. "I hate to admit it, but the Rivals have got it together. And we thought *our* plan was good."

"How could they do all this without help?" Lili asked. "I think Willow was right. Arthur Atkinson must be helping them."

Eli thoughtfully tapped a pen on the table. "Either way, those Rivals kids are pretty smart. You created a distraction for them, and they used it to get the necklace. And since they put back the reproduction, the museum has nothing to investigate. Nice."

Willow looked angry. "I can't believe I handed it right over to them."

"I would have done the same thing," Jasmine assured her. "He really did look like that security guard."

"So what now?" Lili asked. "We know they have the necklace. Can't we try to get it back or something?"

"Isabel's probably sleeping with it under her pillow," Erin said. "But there's no way we can get the police to search the Rivals' houses again. Not after last time."

"So we just give up?" Erin asked.

"And don't forget the formal apology," Jasmine said glumly.

Willow checked the time on her phone. "We'd better do some homework. There's nothing else we can do now, anyway."

There was a sound of shuffling papers as the girls and Eli took books and binders out of their backpacks. Erin groaned and put a small stack of old books on the table.

"I need to take these Martha Washington books back to the school library," she said. "They're heavy."

"But they look so delicate," Lili said, picking up the first book on the stack. "Like they could crumble apart."

She started flipping through the book. "Did you actually read all this? It's like a million words, and the type is so small!"

"Well, not all of it," Erin admitted. As she took the book back from her, a weathered piece of paper fluttered down and landed on the tabletop.

"That looks old," Jasmine remarked.

Erin carefully picked it up. "It *is* old," she said, her eyes wide. "Guys, this is a letter from Martha Washington!"

"No way!" Lili cried, looking over Erin's shoulder.

Willow, Eli, and Jasmine all moved closer to Erin to look at the letter.

Dear Abigail,

It is with great trepidation that I write to you about the four jewels in my possession. At present they are safe, but I believe there are those who know of their significance. The ruby, the diamond, the emerald, and the sapphire are unmatched in beauty, but together . . . I need not tell you what they mean. I have placed the ruby in a necklace and have found a trustworthy jeweler to set the remaining jewels as well. They shall be well hidden.

Your friend,

Martha

"How can we be sure it's from Martha Washington?" Willow asked.

Erin flipped through the book. "See? This photo shows one of her other letters. The handwriting is the same. It's got to be her! I'm totally getting a Martha Washington vibe."

"And who's Abigail?" Lili asked.

"Maybe Abigail Adams," Erin guessed. "She was another first lady. She was married to John Adams. She and Martha might have been friends before independence — before George became the first president and John the first vice president?"

"The ruby, the diamond, the emerald, and the sapphire," Jasmine repeated.

Lili giggled. "Those early first ladies had some serious bling going on!"

"But it didn't sound like Martha was talking about making a fashion statement," Willow pointed out. "She said she was writing with 'great trepidation.' 'Trepidation' means 'fear.'"

"Uh, hello!" Erin rolled her eyes. "We know that. We're on the quiz bowl team with you, remember? But what was she afraid of? Someone stealing the jewels? The British army?"

"I guess if the British army stole them they could sell them and help fund the war," Willow suggested.

"But she was worried about them being found *together*," Jasmine said, thoughtfully. "Wait a second. Do you think she means *our* ruby?"

"I think so," Willow said. "And if Martha was afraid of the jewels being found together, it makes sense that the ruby was part of something bigger, right? Something important?"

Erin nodded. "It certainly sounds like it. So then, where are the other three jewels? And what happens when all four of them are together?"

"I don't know," Willow said. "But I have a feeling that the Rivals might. I thought the ruby theft was just for money, but now I'm not sure."

Everyone was quiet for a moment, until Lili cried out dramatically, "So that means the Rivals will strike again!"

"Unless they already have the other jewels," Eli said. "But if they don't, you could get them first."

Jasmine smiled. "I like that idea."

"Forget about the Rivals," Erin said. "This could be the historical discovery of the century!"

"And while we're at it we can beat the Rivals at their own game — whatever that is, exactly," Lili added.

"Don't forget," Willow reminded them, "we've got to beat them in quiz bowl, too."

Erin frowned. "So let me get this straight. We not only have to become quiz bowl champs, but we've got to put a stop to a bunch of sixth-grade jewel thieves?" A grin slowly spread across her face. "Let's show those Rivals they can't push us around. We'll wipe the floor with them. I'm in!"

Willow smiled and held out her arm. Erin, Jasmine, and Lili each reached out and put a hand on top of hers.

"Come on, Eli," Erin said. "You're part of this, too."

Eli shrugged and put his hand on top of the pile. Then they all gave a cheer in their best library whisper.

"*Goooooo Jewels!*"